GUARDIAN ANGEL

GUARDIAN ANGEL

Comprising
BOOK 1: GHOSTS

BOOK 2: MYSTIC GUARDIAN

Alan Kinder-Cooke

Matador
9 Priory Business Park,
Wistow Road, Kibworth Beauchamp,
Leicestershire. LE8 0RX
Tel: 0116 279 2299
Email: books@troubador.co.uk
Web: www.troubador.co.uk/matador
Twitter: @matadorbooks

ISBN 978 183859 270 7

British Library Cataloguing in Publication Data.
A catalogue record for this book is available from the British Library.

Printed and bound in the UK by TJ International Ltd, Padstow, Cornwall
Typeset in 11pt Aldine by Troubador Publishing Ltd, Leicester, UK

Matador is an imprint of Troubador Publishing Ltd

Dedicated to my wife Hazel for her patience, understanding, and the magic of love; and to all seekers after truth

PRELUDE

THE DOOR
COME NOT Here Before Your TIME
Before You Are CALLED For There
Will Be No Admittance

The words inscribed on the stone seemed stern and forbidding yet the door itself seemed to smile – garlanded with fragrent red roses on climbing vines in which sparrows hopped and chirped happily. What was inside? Wealth, riches, jewels, secrets to obtain fame, wield power, control others? But I knew intuitively, instantaneously, yes I knew. Inside was peace and joy, a sublime ecstatic joy, a joy unthinkable, unfathommable. And I knew with certainty even as I tried the door that it was locked to me. 'You are not ready' said the silent voice in my head. 'I know, I know' I silently replied, and turning stumbled sadly down the steps into the world of time and space. The still small voice called after me 'And when you come again, do not forget to bring the keys.'

Of course, it was just a dream, I think it was a dream.

THE GARDENS OF SOLACE
Locked in my prison of self I sought solitude and

observed life from a distance. Gradually I realised my state and tried to break out. I was forecd to admit my sin of egotism, repent and ask forgiveness. 'Yes' said the small voice, 'you are forgiven – but if you think that is all there is to it, think again. The prison you have built is strong, it will take years of striving to bring it down, perhaps a lifetime to be completely free. You must go into the world and find a path.'

THE INN OF FORGETFULNESS

But the task seemd too great for me. 'The self must die,' the voice had implied. This was going too far. Ridiculous! But the voice did not reply, it had left me. I stayed at the Inn of Forgetfulness for a long time. I may as well loiter along the way and enjoy myself. After all, I would never be capable of opening that door, not for a thousand years. I would still have been there to this day but for a hand that was held out to me. I took hold of the hand just in the nick of time for I was surely drowning in a sea of self-pity and remorse.

THE FLOWER OF LOVE

I held on tight. It was light outside, and there was a path stretching away into the distance. I looked down, and in our clasped hands there was a flower. A flower that unfolded and would never die...

It was just a moment in time
The moment we touched then I knew
Knew we were joined as one
And that our hearts were true

Your life was part of me
My love a part of you
And I was released from selfhood
To live my life anew.

It takes just one moment
To realise this truth
Time exists in selfhood
To the soul it is always now.
It was just a moment in time
The moment we touched then I knew
Knew we were joined as one
And that our love was true.

Many years were to pass before I realised I had been
given a key that had the power to slowly but surely bring
the prison crumbling down, and perhaps the key or one
of the keys to open that door. One day.

BOOK 1

GHOSTS

CONTENTS

INTRODUCTION

During my childhood I became aware of a being, an entity, that existed inside myself. I knew that I was a distinct personality and that this other being was somehow part of me too, but this other was much better than I was. I was rather awful, I was weak and selfish, timid and afraid of others, especially adults. They all seemed to have more confidence and talents than me, and they were also tougher. I compensated for this weakness and timidity by only associating with the kids who were even less confident than me, so I could be the leader and boss them around. This led me to stay rather immature and lacking in social skills. But I think it also led me to somehow converse now and again with this other being inside myself. This other being was my guardian angel.

FOREWORD

A thousand little scientists may come to you and say they have done away with the world of the spirits and even of heaven and hell, but they would be wrong, completely ignorant of the truth. The really great scientists would not and dare not say so. For they know this vast physical universe came from NOTHING, that is "NO THING" because we cannot describe it in physical terms. But this "nothing" existed first and is infinite – the material universe is merely a little bubble in time and space in comparison.

In an analogous way the conscious world in which we live is merely a flow of information from the senses through the network of brain cells in which we think, but there is also perhaps unknown to most of us, a much greater "UNCONSCIOUS" world. You need not take my word for this, but if you need further corroboration I would refer you to the works of Carl Jung.

I propose to take you on a journey from adolescence through to maturity, but not of this physical body but of the mind and soul, the mystic path. Now this sounds rather grave and serious, and I have no wish to seem like a self-righteous Victorian preacher, an attitude that has been rightly denigrated by Charlotte Bronte in Jane Eyre, and by many others since, so let us start off in BOOK I a little light-heartedly with some ghostly tales, and explore the fight between good and evil from a rather obtuse angle. In BOOK I we will just have glimpses of the guardian angel as she lies in the background.

In BOOK 2 the guardian angel is gradually revealed, as I too only came to comprehend her very gradually over the course of many years, and this book will also take us much further along the mystic path to our ultimate destination. I must own that it is really the guardian angel, not me, who guides us along the path.

PROLOGUE

It was the summer of 1972 and the weather becoming quite promising, I took my wife off to Bridlington for a few days. However the resort was pretty busy and after trying a few guest houses without success I was beginning to think we would have to go all the way back to Manchester. Driving to another area of the .town I had one last try. At an attractively built and seemingly fairly large guesthouse. The proprietor who came to the door was a smiling affable man aged about 50. He seemed a little doubtful at first but said he could possibly put us up for one or two days in one of his own rooms, to which I readily agreed. It was late afternoon and they would be busy serving dinner, but he would like to have a chat with us in the lounge later on. We ourselves only wanted bed and breakfast. Also we usually kept to ourselves preferring to be out in the fresh air. However we ventured into the lounge later in the evening and found it to be pretty full with the other guests, who seemed to be mostly middleaged women seated around the proprietor who was sat on a buffet in the middle of the room, regaling them all with stories and anecdotes.

I managed to find a seat for my wife whilst I perched on the arm of her chair. He was a pleasant talking witty chap and they seemed enraptured with him. There was no sign of his wife, and later on another man aged about 40 brought in tea and biscuits. He and the proprietor seemed on very friendly terms. After a while and beginning to get restless I put my arm around my wife's shoulders and in so doing dislodged the closed curtains and something on the windowsill fell over with an ominous tinkling sound, as if it was an expensive china ornament that had just met its doom. I hoped it was not too expensive, and kept quiet about it. Being by now rather warm, embarrassed and restless I made our excuses of being tired and we went to our room. It had two beds – a single one near the window for my wife, and a double one against the further wall for me. This was just right for us, as I am a restless sleeper and need plenty of room! I once slept near an open window during a heat wave and got a muscle spasm in my back that took 3 months before it got better. The bed was soft and comfy and I thought the proprietor had been very good to let us have this room. I fell asleep feeling all right with the world. I woke up about 2a.m. restless and uneasy, then dozed off again. Whether I was asleep, half-dozing or awake I am not sure, but a strong picture came into my mind of this woman with somewhat distraught features who seemed to be urging me to wake up. I could see her clearly, lying in the bed that I now lay in. I had a strong sense of her being smothered by a pillow. I felt her next to me, a very unnerving sensation, then she seemed to say to me, 'He murdered me, to be with his male lover.' I sat up agitated, I had never known this before. What did she want, what could I do? If l went to the police, I had no real evidence. I passed a restless night, and the next morning I said to my wife we are leaving today and finding somewhere else to stay. In the dining room the same chap from the night before served the breakfasts. The proprietor was busy doing the cooking. There was no sign of any women about, apart from the guests. Now all this happened years before people mentioned anything about same-sex relationships. The word 'gay' had not even been coined. Indeed, I had no conception of such matters. Also there was no reason for me to presuppose murder or foul play of any kind. The proprietor had seemed a pleasant and friendly, well-spoken man. I believe the vibrations of traumatic events are left in the 'fabric' of the surroundings. Under certain conditions these vibrations can impinge upon the subconscious mind, and thence filter through to the conscious mind… or perhaps there really are ghosts.

MARIE

It was in the dead of night in the middle of a graveyard that I first met Marie. What was I doing there at that time of night and who the heck is Marie you might ask. Well I will try to tell you, if you will let me, but I'm afraid the beginning is somewhat muddled. It was a Saturday night and I was on this pub crawl to end all pub crawls – alone – because I had quarelled with my two best mates a couple of weeks back and had not spoken to them since – well, you are like that when you are young. I finally staggered out of the last pub on the list, late at night and with little idea in which direction was home – no, I wasn't that drunk – it was just that I had never been so far off the beaten track before and this pub – The Jolly Bargee – was new to me. I think it was alongside a canal or something. However, whatever it was somehow I managed not to fall in the ruddy thing and found myself climbing over this gate and in the middle of this cemetery for two very good reasons. I had some idea it was a short cut and more importantly I needed to relieve myself. Well, I was on the point of doing this when I was suddenly aware of this woman standing among the headstones quietly watching me. I jumped, startled, and I was embarrassed. She did not say anything or move and a sense of fear came over me. Besides which I'd had quite a lot to drink. I mumbled rather stupidly, tripped over an ornament or vase, and somehow found myself back home. When I woke up next morning the main feeling I had was one of embarrassment so, needless to say, I kept well away from that area. Anyway the quarrel was over and most Saturday nights we played snooker at the club.

Eventually I was unable to keep the experience to myself any longer.

"You know what," I said, "I saw a ghost about two weeks ago."

"Sure you did, you looked in the mirror."

"No, it was in that cemetery in Broughton. A woman, a kind of spirit it was, honest."

The mention of a woman made them interested. "What was she like?"

"Dark hair, about thirty five, dressed in black."

"Well there's no such things as ghosts, mate. Probably some widow, putting flowers on a grave."

As the memory of it had become a bit vague I did not pursue the matter, and the subject was dropped.

However that night I dreamed about her. I woke up, and there was a dark figure sitting near the bottom end of the bed. I froze. The seconds ticked by. At last I whispered, "Who are you?" After a minute her reply came to me – 'Marie.' I was not sure whether the word was actually spoken, or if it was a telepathic thought.

"What do you want?"

"We are always looking for others to join us."

"Not me – go away," I said.

She was still there. I sprang up in a kind of panic and dashed for the light switch, waving my arms about. To my relief she had disappeared. 'I must be going loony,' I thought.

Some weeks passed, and I began to feel easier. I suppose I was just glad the immediate problem had gone away. However, I then began to think and wonder. Join them in what? Who were they and what was she? The lads, John and Steve that is, tried to snap me out of it. "You're not concentrating on the game, Frank, giving four points away like that," said Steve disparagingly. "What's the matter with you?"

"Sorry, I was miles away."

"What we need is a bit of life," said John. "Let's try that dance at the Locamo next Friday. It's only a small floor but we might meet some chicks there."

So we went – the usual dimly lit subdued atmosphere, and there were girls there alright. Steve looked around approvingly but both John and I were rather shy when it came to women and we concentrated on our beer, or to be more precise our lager, which we had ordered to try to appear suave and cosmopolitan. Glancing furtively out of the corner of my eye the talent on view did not endear itself to my sensitive nature – tarted up brazen types looking for some free drinks, thrills and kicks, and a one night stand, that's how they seemed to me. Steve was not so bashful; going up to two females sat at one of the tables he asked if we could join them, and called us over. Names exchanged – Wendy and Lisa – and drinks bought and engaging in a bit of awkward banter, we three began to eye each other in a somewhat competitive manner – well there were only two of them! I thought, this girl Wendy ain't bad, and before I could remember I was supposed to be shy, I asked her to dance, which I managed to do after a fashion. I noticed Steve was dancing with Lisa. Not a bad start for an introverted nut like me, but later conversation was a bit awkward and forced and tended to flag. John made a bit of a play for Wendy, which made me rather jealous and sullen.

"We must be going," they said.

"We will walk you home," said Steve. They demurred, put their jackets on, and went off to the powder room.

When I figured it was near time that they would re-emerge. I got up. "Just going to the gents," I said. I had timed it right. "Can I see you again?"

"If you like," she said.

"Outside here. Next Wednesday, half past seven?" We went out together quite a lot after that, but on Saturdays I still played snooker at the club. "You're a dark horse," said Steve. "I fancied her," said John.

"Are you still going out with Lisa?" I asked Steve. "Naw, I've gone off her."

"Let's go on a bit of a pub crawl," said John.

So we took in a few of the pubs, and finished up at The Jolly Bargee. Walking home I foolishly bragged, "Hey, it was just around here I saw that ghost."

"You show me a ghost," said Steve, "and I'll give you five hundred pounds." The offer was tempting, so I took them into the cemetery and we waited – nothing happened. But I was irritated and edgy, why had I taken them, unbelievers, to decry and make fun of my ghost – I knew she was real, I had betrayed her, so my thoughts ran on the way home.

I did not sleep so well, and waking up I knew she was there, sitting in the same place on my bed. Fear coursed through me, yet at the same time I knew I was attracted to her, her quietness and tranquility, and yes – I realised now – I was attracted to her physically. Her dark hair, her dark brown eyes, her cheekbones, her forehead, her lips. Yes, I was attracted to her alright, very strongly indeed; I just hadn't let myself admit it before. Perhaps also, going out with Wendy had woken me up a bit. I got out of bed and sat beside her. Our breathing became audible, at least to me. "Marie," I said, "what do you want?"

"You, if you will." I put my arm around her. She was light, almost insubstantial, small, weak, fragile, feminine. I became uncontrollably sexed up and grabbed her to pull her down on the bed. She disappeared, and I fell down on the bed empty-handed, shocked. I got up, paced to and fro, then calming down a bit got back into bed – it was still very early – half sitting up with my back on the pillow, and tried to think, half dozing. An hour must have passed and opening my eyes, she was there again.

"What happened, why did you go, what are you?"

"Calm down; my dear. All things are composed of vibrations. If you become too physically violent you disturb my vibrations and I am swept off the physical plane. We can love each other if you are gentle."

"But are you a spirit?"

"We are dead, yet alive."

I must say I recoiled at this, and the sensation of fear returned. My mind was in a turmoil, and the thought came 'turn on the light and get away from this', but I loved her. What was love; I wanted her sexually that was certain, I had never been.so aroused before. As I said, my mind was in a turmoil.

"Are you a vampire?" I asked.

"A vampire?" she queried, and I could see the term meant nothing to her, and I was reassured somewhat.

"Well how can you be dead and alive?"

"Most people just live their lives in the conscious mind and brain. But you can live in the subconscious mind if you will. With practice your consciousness can leave the body whilst still maintaining a link with it. If you do this just before death you can live in the spirit like us, and re-materialise the body you last lived in, for you still retain its vibratory essence. For all things, Frank, physical, mental or psychic, are simply composed of vibrations.

"How do you know my name?"

"I read it in your mind. We don't really need words, or even names for that matter."

I became a little disconcerted again, and sensing it she said, "I will leave you now. Call me again when you feel you need me," and she disappeared.

I was all confused. I did not like any of it, but I did not want to lose her, now she had gone I wanted her again. What did she mean 'call her'? I got back to something like normality and concentrated on my work. I also went out with Wendy of course. Wendy was more real, down to earth, although plainer by comparison to Marie. We went rambling together on Sundays and we enjoyed the exercise and the fresh air revived me. I began to say to myself 'keep your feet on the ground, be satisfied with what you've got' Time passed, and I sensed Wendy was expecting our relationship to develop further, and I think this caused me to become a little unsettled, and tossing and turning in bed that night somehow I knew I would see HER. Yes, Marie was there. Had I called?

I gently caressed her, her breasts, her thighs, we kissed and I undressed her. "Be careful," she said, "don't get too carried away." This was very difficult to do because the very injunction added to the excitement, but I was so afraid of losing her again that I managed to control myself sufficiently. During our intercourse I knew I was lost.

"Don't ever leave me."

"Well then you must become one of us."

"How do I do that?"

"It has to be at a special ceremony in a secret place, at the summer solstice."

"Why?" I asked.

"The proper ritual and ceremony are necessary to put you in the right frame of mind, so you may leave the conscious and enter the subconscious. First you must practise certain exercises to familiarise yourself with the process. At nights stop thinking with your conscious brain, make your mind blank and receptive, letting inner visions enter without thinking about them, then even let these disappear as you become just completely blank and become just one with the whole, merged into the whole, with no separate body or consciousness. You will do this for many months before the final ceremony."

I tried to do as she commanded.

I was still unsure about things and the coming 'ceremony' filled me with trepidation. One night I asked her what kind of people entered their world. "People like us, Frank, quiet, thoughtful, introspective. Extraverts are too immersed in the material things and doings of this world."

I was uncertain and not a little fearful as the time drew near when Marie would ask me to undergo the ceremony. What did it entail?

I went out with Wendy for some solace. "I don't see you very often now Frank, why haven't you taken me rambling – the weather's been nice."

"I'm sorry, I've had a lot on my mind."

"It's not just that, you seem more distant now somehow. Tell me what's wrong."

Well, what could I say? All of a sudden the enormity of the situation hit me, I felt lost. I put my head on her shoulder and fought back the tears. She caressed my brow.

"I'm worried about you," she said, "promise me you will see the doctor tomorrow."

"Okay," I replied. We kissed goodnight.

I later found out that Wendy went round to see Steve and John the next day to tell them of her concern for me.

"He's been wrapped up in himself for a while," said Steve. "Probably heading for a nervous breakdown."

"Can't we do anything?"

"Well first you need to find out what's worrying him."

"I asked him, but he couldn't or wouldn't say."

"Not much we can do then."

"You're supposed to be his friends."

"We haven't seen him for a while now."

John said, "We could follow him one night and see where he goes and what he gets up to."

"Well, okay, we could try that, if we get it organised. One of us keeps watch each night positioned near the phone box. If he goes out we ring the others up and follow him. Leave your cars positioned ready in the drive."

It was a few days before they got organised.

Marie was now visiting me every night. I did not need to call her, I was completely in her power.

"It is nearing the time," she said, "don't go out with your acquaintances anymore. It is time for another life."

"But what does this other life entail?"

"You will enter it and be one with me in the ceremony."

"Well what is this ceremony?"

"I cannot tell you any more details or you will not be properly initiated. You are thinking with your conscious mind still, it is time to stop doing that. Just be ready the day after tomorrow. We will drive to a parking place about two miles from the secret place."

"When do we drive back?"

"We don't, I don't think you yet understand, my love." She smiled knowingly, "You won't need the car anymore."

The dreaded day came and I drove in a daze. We parked the car at some lonely country viewpoint up in the hills. I did not want to go but with her beside me I could not help myself. At the trysting place shadowy figures seemed to be formed into a ring around an oblong slab of rock on which they laid me. I did not seem to have any power to resist.

I recall the intonation of some strange vowel sounds. I was told to leave my conscious mind and think only of blankness and death from which I would be reborn. Marie kissed me on the forehead, and I saw a knife descending. Fear and horror suddenly ran through me and jolted me back into consciousness. 'You fool' I thought to myself, 'you've given them your life, the one precious thing you had!'

John was leaning over me and picked me up. Steve and Wendy were dashing about shouting and screaming. They half dragged, half carried me back to the waiting cars.

CIRCLES OF THE OCCULT

"May I kiss you?"

"If you want to."

In that first kiss which seemed to last forever, their past lives faded to nothing, and love was born. Are names really all that important for us ordinary mortals? Her name was Helene, and his Tony, but they rarely called each other by name. She would say, "I love you, hon," and to him she was his 'Princess.'

Tony was a fairly simple kind of guy, who would always support the underdog, and shied away from mundane arguments and any kind of power seeking in the earthly rat race. He knew he had found something beyond price when he fell in love with Helene. A love that grew and strengthened into something much greater than mere sex, a million times more precious than any physical or material possession. Love can be divinely exquisite when it is simple, pure, and guileless.

When she had a heart attack, and was taken from him, he was devastated. How deeply devastated even I, who tells this story, cannot know. For we can never really know how another person feels, except in very general terms. Perhaps this is the way of it, those who are given the greatest joy in love experience the greatest grief – we have to pay for our happiness. I do know he made an attempt to commit suicide, perhaps not in a fully committed way, for he was uncertain what might lie beyond, and at the age of 52 still reasonably young at heart. In this uncertain mood he joined a singles fellowship and met a number of eligible widows, going out with them on tentative dates. Carol even came down to see him staying in a small hotel in the village for three or four days. They enjoyed each other's company, trips to the seaside, and tête-a tête meals in quiet restaurants. In the summer they spent a weeks holiday together. But deep down in his heart he knew nobody could ever replace his Princess, no one could ever possibly, even remotely, replace that magical, intangible, all-powerful love that they had shared.

His sister Anne came down from Scotland to see him.

"You will just have to get used to living on your own again, like Ronnie did. I know that if I lost Eddie that I would never marry again In our family we have all been faithful to one spouse, it's the way we are made, maybe it is our genes."

He knew she was right, but why did not Helene come to him, and console him with some sign? In his loneliness he took to writing poetry, or perhaps I should call them song-poems, for this is an example from many such I found, entitled simply 'I MISS HER.'

O God how I miss her
This parting cannot be endured
The hurt stabs deep in my heart
Deep, deep, deeper than I can bear
Through the burning tears that fall
I will always remember
The love that we did share.
Hear my cry, ye gods and angels
No power on earth will part us
I will love her for ever, ever
Ever, forever to the end of time
In life or in death I must find her
Do battle with the great divide
Till once again my darling... is mine.

It was following this period, and still in this frame of mind, that Tony took to spiritualism. Contacts with mediums, and amateurish manoeuvrings with Ouija boards did not lead him very far however, and he began to study mysticism. To develop oneself along the mystic path, this seemed to point the way to wisdom, light, and understanding. And it gave a meaning to life. The only trouble was that it seemed a long path needing a lifetime to travel, or indeed many lifetimes. And it did not bring him into contact with his beloved.

It was in a large central library that he found the book, bound in black vellum, 'The Seal of Solomon,' attributed to Hermes Trismegistus, which led him to realise there was another world of occult wisdom, hidden from the majority of people, hidden because it was only as the mind and psychic self became developed enough that these occult mysteries could be comprehended. For many years he studied old manuscripts of cabalistic and hermetic magic, including 'THE ZOHAR: The Book of Splendour,' first formulated by Simeon bar Yohai in the 2nd century A.D. and subsequently translated by Moses de Leon; and the writings of Isaac ben Solomon Luria, who described the shards of evil scattered into the universe when a vessel of divine light was shattered just after the Creation. The adept, through meditation and the use of magic formulas, must journey through the seven circles or astral spheres.

It was a dangerous subject to pursue, because it could be fraught with perils. The circles we create keep out the lesser disordered world, and we build an inner citadel of the mind. But this process is only in its infancy for the majority of us, our citadels are weak – indeed most people still exist in the outer chaos, tossed this way and that in its ceaseless churning. And if we stray from our circle and fall into some other – if it be an evil circle then we are lost, in great danger of losing our soul. He lit the candles and placed the crystal orb on the black cloth laid upon his altar, and began to intone the spells to enable him to peer into the beyond.

Black things that seemed able to change their shapes and their features at will, emanated forth from the crystal. Beings that had power, power to will things to happen or come into existence by thought only – things that would come to pass below, or in their own dark domain, but not above. They stood him before them, how he did not know, as if to judge or appraise him. Their power and their evil was far beyond his grasp or comprehension.

As if in answer to his unspoken question, he heard one of them say:

"There is a White Brotherhood, but you will not find it here – you have come to us. Once you have come to us and have seen us you cannot leave the Cabalistic circle, for that is one of the laws of the arcane and occult mysteries. Did you not understand these things when first you tampered with our rites?"

"No," he pleaded, "all I want is to see my wife."

The voice, commanding, came again to him: "Now that you have seen us we cannot permit you to leave our circle."

"I do not understand, how can that be, are we not in different worlds?"

Fingers of darkness began to probe into his mind, and with a sudden horror he knew they were going to take him to their evil abode – but his body would be left – lifeless on the floor.

Doctor Hassler

There comes a time in everybody's life when they must face up to their nemesis, and here was I being compelled to do so. A lingering and painful illness was in prospect before my inevitable death. Doctor Hassler was sympathetic. "Have you any relatives?" he asked, among the other questions he threw at me after the examination. "In your case," he said, "euthanasia is a course worth considering. Quite a few of my patients opt for it nowadays. It's quite painless and will ease your passage out of this world of travail and into the next." He smiled encouragingly, and raised his thick bushy eyebrows as if he was pressing me for an answer there and then.

"Well, all right, if you think it would be best," but I wasn't at all sure about it and regretted my rash answer. I felt that I had been pressured into it. His smile broadened as if in gleeful anticipation and my doubts increased. What did I really know about this man, could I trust him with my life, or perhaps I should say my death? He had only been in the practice about six months.

I was a rather timid chap, and I got up to go, feeling

I needed time to think, and to escape. But he detained me with a little gesture and writing quickly on a form, he asked me to sign it. He had a commanding presence and made you feel inferior, as if he possessed knowledge of life's processes, of the workings of the mind and body, far beyond your own, and therefore must obey his superior wisdom – or acquiesce to his overbearing personality. He had rather a large head and face, probably of Austrian or German extraction, and he made you feel weak, puny, and insecure. I thought 'pity the poor bugger who goes to him for psychological help, he would make them feel ten times worse.' I could not prevail over his intense gaze and I meekly signed. I knew that I had signed away my life! I wanted to get away, to run, to escape, both from him and from my wony and fear.

"See the nurse on your way out to book another appointment," he said. But I went out quickly, in a daze.

The next day the telephone rang. "Mr. Andrews? This is the doctor's receptionist, and you need to make another appointment."

"I'm sorry," I mumbled, "I've changed my mind."

"Doctor Hassler says you really need to see him again for proper treatment of your condition."

"I'm sorry, but I feel okay now, and I'm going away this week," I lied. "I will see him another time."

"Very well, Mr. Andrews. Get in touch when you return, will you?"

I put the phone down. I felt pursued. I unplugged the phone, locked the door, and did not go out for a week. The interview with Doctor Hassler had scared me so much I did not notice my illness for some time, but then the symptoms reappeared again, prostate pain, long protruding haemorrhoids, urinary incontinence – I won't go into more details. But it made me want to put an end to it all, as I could not bear to be a burden on other people in that condition. I made out a Will, although I did not have all that much to leave, a widower with no children, nearest relatives living half way round the world, and for a while I toyed with the idea of suicide. But I finally had to admit I lacked such courage.

A couple of months passed and I made another appointment at the doctors.

"How are you now? Better or worse?" he asked. "You did not return for your previous appointment."

"I was hoping that I might get better, or you could perhaps find a cure."

"Well you can go through varying periods of remission, but I cannot promise you any more than that, I'm afraid. I will prescribe some different tablets for you to try. But you must make your own decision as to when you decide to end it. I'm afraid there is not much else that I can do for you. Make another appointment on your way out."

The tablets made me worse, sick and dizzy, and I returned to keep the appointment. "I'm ready," I said.

"Good, just go into the next room, roll up your sleeve, and relax. You will just drift off to sleep, quite quickly."

He came in a few minutes later. "Could you lie on here, please," indicating a trolley contraption. He then gave me the injection. But I did not sleep. I just felt paralysed, unable to move. Time passed, doors slammed, it became quiet, and went dark.

Hassler came in some time later, and wheeled the trolley out through a back door into a private car park. It was dark outside and the fresh air felt cool on my face. He dragged me off the trolley into the back of a large estate car, and went back inside for a few minutes. The drive took about forty-five minutes, when he transferred me on a stretcher into a rather large private house, all the while pulling the stretcher along by two of its handles, on his own. He did not speak or pay any regard to me, or the bumps I received. I realised he was utterly indifferent to me as if I was just a piece of flesh to him, and completely in his power – or did he think I was dead?

I was transferred to a kind of trestle bed, simply elastic strips stretched across a metal framework, then he left me although I could still hear him moving around somewhere, but not see him, my eye muscles still being paralysed. Much later he came to me, and clamped my wrists and ankles to the frame. At last he spoke to me, "You will lose the paralysis before long, and I will be busy at the surgery till tomorrow evening, so I must secure you I'm afraid," was all he said.

The paralysis did leave me the next morning and I could view my surroundings. I was in a large laboratory filled with a great deal of equipment. Five other bodies were laid on trestles, they did not move or speak, and I assumed they were probably dead: The horror of my situation was almost beyond enduring.

I heard a key tum in a lock somewhere, and at last he appeared.

"What's going on?" I demanded.

"Try not to worry too much, Mr… Andrews isn't it? You will not feel much pain, but you see I have important research work to do, and I need human bodies to do my kind of experiments. You see I am interested in mapping the genes of human personality, and how that personality can be altered and manipulated."

"You mean you butcher and dissect people for your own ends."

"My dear sir, you offend me. The pursuit of science and of knowledge is an end in itself, although it may well have possibilities in its application that is true. You may however be glad to know there is nothing seriously wrong with you, and I must admit that I misled you to think and feel that there was, in order to obtain the use of your body – you see there is no other way I can do my research."

"What do you intend to do with me?"

"You would not understand, and I do not have the time to explain the details. By splicing pieces of DNA material into brain cells I have been able to alter a person's concept of themselves, or in common parlance their personality."

"You will be found out, and what have you done with these others. You have murdered them."

"No, they are not dead, not yet. They are in suspended animation. Periodically I awaken them and continue my observations. I used to have to freeze them, but I have found a better method of semi-suspension using a paralytic drug. They do die eventually. I have their authority for euthanasia of course, as I have yours, and deliver a body to the crematorium as becomes necessary. However do not worry, I do not intend to kill you. You see my research has now progressed beyond experimentation and observation, and I can give you a new personality, and eventually you will be free to go and live as you wish, for you will have forgotten all about your past life. That is, if all goes to plan of course."

The whole thing was a nightmare, but at least apparently he did not intend to kill me. If I managed to get out alive I would denounce him.

"I need some food," I said.

He considered a moment. "I will free one of your hands and get you something, as I am not yet ready for you. But soon you will have to survive on a glucose and saline drip, during your periods of suspension, and until the change is complete."

A week went by. Every morning and evening the trestle was raised almost vertically on a lever and spring system so that ablutions could be performed.

Then one evening he approached with a syringe, and after injection consciousness left me. The next thing I remember was waking up to find my head in bandages and a drip feed in my arm. He came over to me.

"How are you?" he asked. I did not reply.

"The next time I operate you will wake up paralysed, I'm afraid it is better that way for the genetic cells to multiply, and also as far as looking after you is concerned, so I am telling you this now so you will be aware of the situation. It will probably take about ten weeks altogether. But try not to worry, it is in my own interests, for the success of my experiments, that you survive."

I do not remember any more.

Doctor Hassler awakened the patient "How are you?"

The man on the trestle bed looked non-plussed.

"Where am I?"

"You have just recovered from an operation, but hopefully you will be fine in a couple of days. What is your name?"

The man was silent for a while. "I don't know," he said.

"From our records your name is Peter Johnson. Try to remember that, won't you. You must stay under observation for a while. We must see what you can remember later on. We can provide you with a room to stay here for a while until you are fully recovered, then you can register with the authorities, and find employment."

Dr. Hassler smiled.

"That is very nice of you," said Mr, Johnson.

Some weeks passed and Doctor Hassler came to visit him. "Well Peter, if you have not got a job yet, how would you like to work for me here. I do quite a lot of work here nowadays, in my laboratory in the west wing, and I could do with some help."

"Yes, that would suit me fine. I have often fancied doing medical work, and operations and that," he answered, and his eyes gleamed eagerly. "I can't wait to get to work."

Hassler beamed, "I've certainly changed his personality," he thought to himself..

Peter was an apt pupil, and was soon preparing DNA cultures, and injecting the 'patients', and even assisting with the operations. One evening Doctor Hassler came into his laboratory, and much to his surprise found his assistant already there.

"How did you get in?" he asked angrily.

"I had a spare key made, so I could get more work done."

"You had no right."

"I've got everything prepared for you."

"How do you mean, you do not know my plan of work."

"Over here." he pointed, and Hassler bent his head to look past him.

Just then he felt a prick, a little stab of pain in his neck. Peter had an hypodermic syringe in his hand. Horror came on the doctor's face as he felt paralysis creeping over him.

"By the way, doctor, my name isn't Peter Johnson. You must have a bad memory – it's Derek Andrews."

RITES OF THE DEAD

Gordon was twelve years old when he was taken on a school visit to the Manchester Museum. Hundreds of paintings, sculptures, old ornaments and tapestries passed before his gaze, and the school party proceeded on its merry way, when he saw a darker side room and slipped into it. He was immediately enthralled by the sight of much more ancient artefacts. A strange sense of quiet seemed to brood over the room. He walked further in and coming to a far comer he suddenly saw them and stepped back in awe, frightened. There were three mummies laid out in various positions, one laid in a kind of stone coffin; he had never actually seen one before, never been this close to ancient mystery. And what could be under those ragged brown bandages, was there a real body, was it still alive, it was horrible yet fascinating to him and he gazed at them for a long time, transfixed. Then he realised he was lost in that big building and had little idea how he would get home. He hurried out and after traversing some corridors and rooms was fortunate to regain the school party on its way to the exit.

At the age of twenty four his firm sent him to work

in the London branch for about three months. Whilst there he decided to visit the British Museum and once more his footsteps led him to the Egyptian Antiquities and here his heart fairly leaped with excitement. The room was vast, and there must have been at least thirty of them, some stood up vertically in their coffins, most laid out in semi-horizontal positions. He was fascinated, here he could spend all day just looking at and examining them. Some of the bandages were clean and of a creamy colour as if the museum officials had cleaned them up or put new wrappings on them, which puzzled him. But on others they were tattered and discoloured, a dirty brown, and these intrigued him and also scared him a little. Was that discolouration dried blood he wondered. What was actually under those bandages and what were they for? How could they preserve a body for four thousand years, it was incredible. Was it just crumbled dust under them? He spent hours looking at them, before returning to Manchester.

Back in Manchester he had a chat with his workmate James Wolfson, who had only been with the firm about a year. He was an egotistic chap, who seemed to regard himself as above the common herd, as somehow different to others. It was probably due to this characteristic that although he would tolerate 'Jim' he flew into a rage if anybody called him Jimmy. Gordon regarded him as vain and slightly vindictive, and a bit mad, and yet he got along with him alright in other respects – we are all a mixture of good and bad traits. James was interested in anything abnormal especially if it could help to raise him up in the eyes of others. However at first he did not show much interest in the subject.

"I should imagine it is only dried skin stretched over a skeleton of bone by now. From what I know about it they dragged out the entrails through the anus, and the brains through the nose, then poured embalming fluid all over it."

"You mean there's no proper body in there, it's a bit of a fraud then," said Gordon, feeling cheated and not a little disgusted. "Those ancient embalmers then were duping their fellow citizens, even their kings and pharaohs, for centuries. Didn't they believe the body would rise up again after death and travel over the river Horus or Styx so as to attain immortality?"

"Well, you could always read up more about it, they probably have books in the Central Library on the subject."

In the coming weeks Gordon did read up on it, although he would most likely not have done so without that little push from James. What he found out restored his fascination with mummies, and when he next spoke to James he found that he too had delved into it, and was now deeply interested. They pooled their information. The ancient Egyptians used embalming, in which they had become experts, as a means of preparing the dead for the life after death, and the practice spread to the Assyrians, Scythians, Jews and Persians. On being unwrapped the mummified bodies are still soft and elastic after as much as three thousand years. The embalming process consisted essentially of the removal of the brains and viscera, and the filling of body cavities with a mixture of bituminous substances, balsamic herbs, aromatic spices, and salt. For those of high class, status, or wealth the viscera were immersed in an embalming fluid and then replaced in the body. They also immersed the body in carbonate of soda, injected the arteries and veins with balsams, then wound cloths saturated with bitumen, tar and wax around the body.

"The bodies are intact then," said Gordon.

"Yes, it would seem so. It's very interesting, they seemed to believe that if they preserved the body it could live on in another world, or at least that the soul of the person would live on, a strange and weird subject – fascinating."

A look of excitement and desire had come over James' face, a mad dream of immortality.

One day during their lunch break James said. "I wonder what it is like to cross over to the other world – if any of them ever did."

Gordon was sceptical, "It was just an ancient belief."

"Ancient knowledge that has become lost to the world, that is what interests me. How about a weekend in London, Gordon – I will pay if you will come with me. I would like to visit that museum you told me about. you know where it is. And we could visit the Planetarium, take in a show, anything you like."

"Well okay, Jim, sounds alright to me, if you can just pay for the fares there and back."

They agreed to go on the Friday morning and stay till Sunday night.

"Did you know that they believed the Ka, the soul or vital life force, was a duplicate of the physical body, existing on the psychic plane. After death the soul may eventually depart and take its place in the kingdom of the dead, but this can involve several stages and take a very long time, so it is necessary to keep the corpse intact until the resurrection is achieved – you see the Ka and the body cannot exist without each other on this plane. Osirus himself was mummified by his sister-wife Isis, with the help of the god Anubis, and was later resurrected and became king of the netherworld. Horus, their son, became king of the earth, god of the sky, and of light and goodness."

"I knew Horus came into it somewhere," replied Gordon.

In London they visited the museum on the Friday and James was enthralled, "It's fantastic!" he exulted, "and look at this." He dragged Gordon over to one of the coffins, where on the breast of the enclosed mummy was laid a thick papyrus parchment folded like a book with hieroglyphic characters inscribed on it. On the wall above they saw an explanatory notice:

THE BOOK OF THE DEAD

After leaving the tomb the souls of the dead could be beset by many dangers, and the tombs were therefore furnished with a copy of The Book Of The Dead, a guide for the soul's journey in the underworld, which contained charms designed to protect the Ka on this journey, together with other magical formulas, hymns and prayers. After arriving in Amenti, the region of the dead, the Ka was judged by Osiris, the king of the dead, and his 42 assistant judges. The Book Of The Dead also contains instructions for the proper conduct before these judges. If the judges decide that the deceased had been a sinner the Ka was condemned to hunger and thirst or to be tom to pieces by demons. If the decision was favourable the Ka would go to the heavenly realm of The Fields of Yaru.

"I have always found all this very strange and interesting," opined Gordon, although he was also a little disconcerted to find that James now seemed to be more into it and informed than he was.

In the hotel that night James revealed his intentions. "I want to examine one of those mummies more closely," he said. Actually he was planning to take off the wrappings and see just what was underneath. "The only way I might do it is to secrete myself somewhere before they lock up for the day."

"They probably have security guards," said Gordon. "Well, I can always say I got locked in, anyway I don't think they can afford the manpower these days. What they do is record how many people go in, and they give you a tag card which you have to deposit at the exit – I'm not sure what this is for, it probably tells them how long you remained inside. As you push the exit turnstile it clicks round and mechanically records the number going out, also your body breaks a beam of light about waist level and a photo-electric cell records it electronically."

"You can do it on your own, can't you. I want to do some shopping tomorrow, and maybe see a show."

"I only need you to go in with me, and then you can go out and do what you want. You go through the exit as normal, I will be close behind but I'm not going through; you can't push the turnstile strongly enough from the inside so I need you to pull it from your side so that it clicks round, and at the same time I will put my arm over so that it breaks the beam. Then I hope to hide myself somewhere amongst the exhibits. If it does not work or I am spotted I will just bluff it out and say I lost my card."

"Well okay, it's your funeral, but I have just thought of a snag."

"What's that?"

"You will probably be locked in till Monday morning, and we are due back at work."

"Yes I know, but that can't be helped. I will have to take the day off that's all. I will see you Tuesday and let you know how I got on."

"But what about food and drink?"

"We could have a good meal Saturday afternoon – you could do your shopping first. We will go in about an hour before closing. I will take a flask and a sandwich to tide me over till Monday."

The plan worked, after a fashion, in that James was able to secrete himself in a small side room, and late on Saturday night he came out of hiding. It was pitch black, there were no windows, a circumstance he had not considered, although he had a small pencil torch. The light from it was not all that great however, illuminating a small one-inch diameter circle, and if he held it further away to try to see more it just made vague dark shadows dance all over the place. He went over to one of the corpses, and began fumbling about with the bandages. They were very dry and creaked and crackled at his touch, and there seemed to no end to the task. it was difficult to see what he was doing. He was sweating with anxiety that he might be discovered. and also with fear of the unknown. As he proceeded he could feel a body underneath the wrappings and his hand touched some sticky substance, and he shuddered. And now a sickly odour oozed from the corpse, partly sweet and aromatic yet at the same time partly putrid. He was tired. Perhaps it would be best to wait till morning, it might be a bit lighter, and he had plenty of time, hadn't he. He lay down on a carpet some two metres from the mummy, and tried to get some sleep.

In the night he felt something pressing on his chest, some thing seemed to be clambering to get inside him. He slapped his hand to his chest in fright, there was nothing there but the feeling persisted, some strange substance or something intangible was upon him. He shivered and sat up quickly opening his mouth in horror and it seemed to slide down his throat. He got up, startled, fearful, what was it, what had happened. A feeling of panic sweeping over him made him feel ill. He stumbled to the door but it was locked. He turned round and shone his torch. Threatening shadows danced about the room, but gradually his fear subsided. He felt weak and ill, and lay down again on the floor. But he was unable to sleep, and be did not feel right, something was wrong. He felt strange, different, not himself anymore.

They found him on Monday morning, exhausted and with a look of fear on his haggard face. He was detained, asked for his name and address. An attendant came back to the desk and quickly spoke to an official –

the opened mummy had been discovered. The official called the police, then came over to him. He listened in a daze as he was told that he would be charged with damaging a museum exhibit.

It was a week before Gordon saw him again at work. He looked apathetic and ill at ease.

"Are you alright, Jim?"

"I've lost interest in this job, Gordon. I think I will pack it in at the end of the week, have a rest. Come over to see me sometime, won't you."

"What happened at the museum?"

"Oh, nothing. I got caught on the premises and had to go to court."

James duly gave in his week's notice. He lived in a flat, out near Sale, on his own. Gordon went over to see him about three months later. He looked terrible.

"Hello, Gordon, glad to see you."

"How are you," asked Gordon, out of politeness but he could tell he was not well. James looked as if he was suffering from a nervous breakdown.

"We've all got to die sometime. But Amon-Ra, god of the sun, and Osiris, can give us immortality. That is what I am seeking now, and I think I have found it. But it's not the flesh and the body that is important, they've got it all wrong, it's the spirit."

Gordon tried to humour him, he knew Jim could become a bit difficult when aroused.

"How about coming out for a drink?"

"My days of going out are over. Look, Gordon, when I was in that museum I became enlightened, new knowledge came into me. I do not bother with the passing paltry things of this world now. I can give you this knowledge too if you will join me."

"Join you? In what?"

"To be one with the Pharaohs. We must worship their gods – Amon, Thoth and Ptah will aid us."

Gordon looked at him. James' skin had become yellow and wrinkled like parchment. And his mind must be crumbling. Either that or he had been taken over by something, or maybe he was infected with some disease. He was ageing before his time. James saw the shock and pity on Gordon's face.

"I think I am going to die soon, but either I or some Egyptian spirit will live on," Here he broke down and wept.

"I suppose it is my own fault, it's what I deserve. Beware, Gordon." Gordon made some hurried excuse about having to get back home, and made his exit.

He went to the funeral. There were not many there. At the house James' body was laid out on view in the coffin. Gordon bent over it to pay his last respects – it seemed the proper thing to do. As he did so some air that must have been trapped in the lungs or the stomach was expelled. He stepped back in revulsion, inadvertently gasping and sucking in his breath.

As he went out he thought 'serves the bugger right, for being so vainglorious, he would shoot you down in flames if you so much as contradicted him, and the poor sap must have gone off his rocker in the end.'

He coughed, some mucus seemed to have got stuck on his chest, a touch of indigestion perhaps.

SORAYA

Soraya was no ordinary ghost, for she appeared to me in the night in my dreams. Tall, majestic, a great power and radiance shone from her so that all else seemed dark. If I tried to tum away she was still there before me, all pervasive, and I knew it was useless to try to escape. I put out my arm in an hesitant attempt to touch her or ward her off, and asked "What do you want?" My hand tingled and I withdrew it, and she replied, "It is time for you to make decisions, to determine where you are, to stand up and be counted one way or the other." I did not know what to say.

My thoughts seemed to be torn between two opposing forces. Then I was drawn to an easy path lying before me, that offered to gratify my desires – the physical desire for sexual pleasure, and the mental desire for self-aggrandisement. I went down this path, and fell asleep dreaming of sexual encounters.

When I awoke next morning I had a faint recollection of this dream, and I sensed that I had somehow failed, I had been tested and had been found wanting.

A long time afterwards she appeared to me again

and in answer to my unspoken questions she said, "I am Soraya, angel of life and death. If I chose I could appear to all mankind simultaneously and lead them to wheresoever I wished, even to their final death and annihilation, if that was my will. Do you not realise this is so? But that is not my will, my purpose is to give Life, if you are able to receive it. Do you understand this?"

I know now that it is so. For she has visited me a number of times – but I always failed the test. But over the years I have learnt some things. It was not sex itself that was being tested but my own mind, its weakness and its perversity. The flesh is weak and needs a strong mind to control it, but where can a strong mind come from, when, if like me, you are forever vacillating with no set goals, ideals, or moral strength? I think I have at last, too late in the day, come to know the answer.

Last night I saw her again, perhaps for the last time. Somehow I knew it was my last chance – and I also knew that I would most likely fail.

"Tell me what I must do," I pleaded.

A picture of a golden cross appeared in my mind. "Look into the intersection of this cross," she said.

At first I saw nothing, but perhaps because of her presence my mind was filled with a sense of beauty, of a nurturing love, of reverence for things above and beyond me, and in this meditation a rose appeared, a deep red rose of exquisite form and texture, and slightly unfolding it pierced my heart with its tranquility, its acceptance. It did not desire. It just was. It was my soul.

It was then that I threw away all desire, and suddenly for the first time in my life I knew what purity was. I woke up feeling refreshed. But if I have at last passed this initial test will this new phase last very long? Knowing myself like I do probably not – and I have a strong presentiment that it is too late. I do not know what it all means, perhaps I am just an idiot, or it is all my imagination. I have simply presented these few facts relating to my encounters with Soraya in the hope that it may be of help to someone more mentally mature than myself, someone capable of understanding – someone who stands at the crossroads and waits.

Soraya is a spirit, who comes in dreams, but she is real – more real maybe than you or I. It is perhaps we that live in a dream world, and in the night in our subconscious minds we catch a glimpse of reality.

INTERLUDE
(Editorial Musings)

Most of the events in these little tales occurred long before the present era of technological advances such as mobile phones and the widespread use of CCTV cameras, computers, etcetera and these stories just relate the bare details, for I prefer a concise non-wordy style.

When space and time were created then finiteness came into being, and when life was created death came too. When light was created then darkness came into being. And when good was created then evil also came into existence. In Chinese philosophy this is the yin and yang of existence. Evil is extant therefore in the universe, but it also resides within us, that is in our own minds. This comes about from the metaphysical principle that man is the microcosm of the universe, the macrocosm.

The final goal of any ghosts, and for us also, is to be at peace. This Peace is attained by only one commandment: Love.

O, if l could but embrace thee!

Hidden in this little book, like plants growing out of soil, or man ascending from the apes, or pearls amidst the dross, are the keys to open the Door, the keys of heaven, guarded by the goddess of wisdom. This leads me to introduce to you Sophia. I did not invent Sophia, for I am sure she is real – I am merely a channel through which a small part of her story has been obscurely revealed. I do not comprehend her fully for I claim no distinction above my fellows, and you may come to understand and know her better than I do.

Though you may not believe now, some day you will come to know.

A. K-C.

SOPHIA

In my dreams I see you, Sophia
Dark, threatening, mysterious
Whence you came I do not know
Except you are, and all heads must bow.

SOPHIA

CHAPTER 1

Perhaps you have never seen a ghost – but I have, and the experience was far from pleasant. I hope I do not offend the reader with my tale, for it is true, every detail is indeed true. I was 25, single, and I suppose I did not take life very seriously. I rather frittered it away, in other words. I was walking home alone in the dead of night along this canal path. It was late and so I had chosen on this route to cut a bit off the distance, even so I had about a mile and half to go along the canal and another mile along the road before I was home. It was very dark, very quiet and still, except for now and again a glimmer of light reflected in the water when the moon met a gap in the clouds. Naturally I was a bit uneasy – you get to imagine some assailant springing upon you out of the shadows. I wish now that I had taken the long way round. The path led past some kind of water purification plant with two circular filtering beds with slowly rotating arms over them. It had once been an old cemetery and about a dozen neglected small headstones poked crookedly from the ground on the far side behind the fence of wire netting circling the works. I did not give them much thought. But just as I was nearly past this place I was startled out of my skin by this woman stood almost directly in my path. But I became even more afraid as I began to slowly realise that she was a ghost – silent and still she was, seeing me yet seeing through me, a deathly white translucent pallor to her skin, like marble. Fear and panic swept through me. I could not get past very well on the narrow canal path even if I had had the courage to brush past her, which I certainly hadn't. I turned and ran. God what a nightmare, I didn't stop running till I was out of breath and had to slow up, but I staggered on till I was back on the main roads. Being very late there was nobody about, not even a car, but I felt a bit easier and paused to get my breath. Don't panic, I said to myself. Even if it really was a ghost they can't hurt you, can they? They are just disembodied spirits who have found no resting-place. Reasoning thus I calmed down a bit and trudged the long way home.

But I was never quite the same after that – would you be? I never went there again, not at night. However about two years later I got this job at the plastics factory, which adjoined the canal on the other side – I worked in the laboratory. I could get two buses home or I could cross a bridge and walk along the canal. A few people used the canal as a short cut to get to the industrial estate although most of these cycled it. Naturally the temptation to save money overcame my reluctance and made me opt for the canal walk. And all went well, till late November when it began to go dusk about 4 o'clock. On the way home from work one evening – it would be around quarter past five – I became suddenly nervous and sensed she was waiting for me. I looked fearfully ahead but all was clear. Then glancing to the side I saw her – she was about 40 yards off to the side, standing still amongst some scrub-land, looking at me. I hurried on hoping I might get by unmolested. She did not move and I breathed more easily. I took the bus for a while, then at the beginning of March decided to use the path again.

On the second day I saw her again, only ten yards away, even though it was still fairly light – dusk was just beginning to gather. She beckoned, and I walked almost transfixed towards her.

"Come with me and I will gratify all your desires, for I possess the power to do this," her thought came to me. Dark evil thoughts filled my mind, and I backed away, and somehow managed to tear myself away.

That night I was restless and could not sleep. I had tried not to think of her but it was impossible. The picture of her came into my mind. She was beautiful in a way, attractive, alluring, dark hair, dark violet eyes, in a black nun-like habit.

"Come with me, Paul, and I will make all your secret desires come true, let your senses run riot, you can do what you will with no retribution, for I am the Arbiter, all is subservient to my will, in my land of shadows."

As she spoke images came unbidden into my mind – or they came from my mind, I know not which – evil images of cruelty and power, lust and depravity – and

I wanted to possess her, above all else I wanted her, to violate her, to ravish her, still in her nun's gown, with that angelic smile upon her face, her lips parted, to die in incessant carnal intercourse with her, till I was lost in her land of shadows. I sat up sweating with fear.

'It was just a dream, or a nightmare, wasn't it?' I said to myself. I did not go to work the next day – instead I went to the doctors.

Then I was referred to a psychiatrist at a local hospital. There were days of questions, and courses of tablets, but I did not really feel that they comprehended the situation. My friends, mainly local lads that I had grown up with, urged me to snap out of it. At nights I would have these dreams of her. I have not been to work for some months now. They say I have had a nervous breakdown.

CHAPTER 2

Since writing the foregoing there have been other developments. In August I was put in touch with a priest, the reverend John Hughes, who I went to see at his rectory on the outskirts of Rochdale. Well actually he shared this rectory with the parish priest, a Father Dawson; apparently he himself has a roving commission to exorcise demonic spirits. Although I did not believe in what I considered to be outdated mumbo-jumbo I went along to see him as arranged. After telling him my story he said, "In order to exorcise this restless spirit we must go to the spot she frequents and wait for her to appear. Only then may I abjure the spirit to depart from this earthly plane."

"And what if she chooses not to appear?"

"I think she will, from my experience and work in this area I think they must. Not everybody can see them, people completely immersed in the hurrying activities of this material world are unlikely to see them. You, on the other hand, are perhaps a more thoughtful introspective type of person and are therefore more sensitive and receptive to their vibrations – to you she has appeared, and hopefully to me for I have made a study of this subject. However, even if I am unable to actually see her I can still perform the exorcism as long as you can show me where she is."

"Good, but I wish she had chosen someone else and not me to appear to."

The rectory was set in a large garden surrounded by some woodland. I looked out of the study window. Rooks or jackdaws – I never could tell which – were circling the tall trees, making their harsh croaks and caws. It sounded soothing. It was early September and the garden was pleasant and peaceful.

"Now I am here I'm beginning to relax," I said.

"Well that's a start," he laughed good-naturedly. "Let's hope I can sort this matter out for you. If you feel you need someone to talk to you are welcome to come and visit me, but give me a ring first. Father Dawson and I have a morning secretary cum tea lady, give her a ring. Then there is the church here, you can always go in the church, and look round the grounds and gardens for some peace and quiet."

He consulted his diary. "Now to get back to the business in hand. Next Wednesday September 15th is convenient. I usually come down to the scene, and stay for up to a week. However, in this case as Chadderton is not that far away, I think I can stay at my base here. Well, I will come down on September the 15th then and call for you at your home at 3 o'clock – now you live at Old Moston, which is next door to Chadderton I believe – is that right?"

"Yes," I replied. "Does it have to be dark?"

"No, I do not think so. It is just that usually these things are more visible in the dark. We will see how it goes. That is why I allow three or four days for a visitation. Right, that's arranged then – I will see you then, Mr. Thompson. What is your first name by the way?"

"Paul." We shook hands.

Father John called for me as arranged. "Well, how are you, my boy?"

"Not too bad, I haven't been troubled since I came down to see you."

"Good, good. Things look promising then."

Actually, I was thinking that perhaps now I was feeling better it might be best to leave things alone, and call it off. I certainly did not want to revive those memories. However now that he was here and it had all been arranged I kept quiet.

I directed him to a convenient parking place where we could access the canal, and we proceeded to the dreaded place. We walked off the canal path and forced our way through some old dilapidated fencing and a hedge to the scrub-land where I had last seen her.

The priest said, "We must now be quiet and wait. I will conceal myself behind a bush over there. When you see her raise your left hand."

We had waited nearly an hour when she suddenly appeared to me just two yards away. This time she did not fill my mind with images but merely looked at me questioningly, searchingly. I raised my hand, and John walked up quite quickly, on the palm of his right hand he had a bible, while his left hand held a book of prayer up from which he was reading some admonition and abjuration. After five minutes of this she disappeared and John heaved a sigh of relief

"How do we know it has worked?" I asked.

"We will have to come again, on at least two more occasions – to make sure."

I was a bit disconcerted at this. "Can't you go alone, I think she is calling me, just before she left she told me her name was Sophia. I have a strange feeling that she has not gone, and I would sooner keep away."

"Well it would be best if we both came again tomorrow, to make sure."

That night I dreamt of her.

Everywhere was black, a deep opaque black. Then she appeared, or rather her face and hands appeared for her dress was black. She smiled and held out her arms to me; "I love you, Paul, do you not love me?"

"Yes, of course I do, for I know you come to fulfil my desires. I have only to think of you and you come to me, your power enters into me so that I in tum may fulfil your desire. What do you wish from me, Sophia."

"Bow down to me and serve me, is not your will subservient to mine, do I not possess thee?"

"Yes Sophia, oh yes Sophia."

And in this dream I ejaculated in an ecstasy both of desire and surrender.

The next day, by the canal with John, was a repeat of the first occasion, only this time John did not bother to conceal himself. When we got back to the car I said, "You had best go on your own next time, John. I am afraid of her."

"Yes, she has a strange power," he said.

"My fears are coming back – and I think there were more than just her there."

"I did not see any others. I certainly did see her though, Paul, so I can assure you that you are not going mad or hallucinating. But for some reason the exorcism does not seem to have worked, and if there are others then it worries me. I may not be able to handle this situation."

John Hughes' self-esteem had been hurt by his apparent failure, but it was more than that. The apparition had made him afraid although he did not want to admit it, afraid of her and of his own thoughts. To ease these fears I think he subconsciously sought to shift the cause of the phenomenon onto me.

He went on, "There is a Doctor of Psychology I sometimes have contact with in difficult cases. I will bring her in on this, I think."

"How can she help?"

"I don't know, Paul," he said irritably, "these things are very deep, too deep for me sometimes. Perhaps you and your mental condition are somehow involved."

"I thought you said I was not going mad."

He shuffled his feet. "Well, it's not that," he said, "but it might be that you bring her forth – from the beyond. It is all a bit complicated, and there is little more I can do. If you will just see this doctor she may be able to help."

A sense of unease seemed to have come over the Reverend, and he looked worried. "In the meanwhile remember that you can always come over and visit me." He started the car. "I must be off and do some studying," he mumbled, more to himself than to me. I was to learn later that some of the people he saw were psychologically unbalanced and he had become accustomed to passing these cases on for psychiatric help.

Two nights later I had this dream. I say dream, but it was more than just a dream for I was still awake, restless, lying in my bed. It was a visitation, not a dream....

Her dark eyes glistened as she looked at me. "You fear me, do you not?" she said, "for I have power, and what I will is. Come to me and I will share it with you."

"Who are you?"

"I am Sophia, do you not want to belong to me, do you not want to be mine?" I did not answer. A fear came on me, a fear that if I died in my present state of mind that I would become like unto one of them. From that moment I seemed to be trapped in a land of shadows. I felt pursued. My mental and physical health began to deteriorate, and I went over to see John Hughes.

CHAPTER 3

"Hello Paul," he said as he opened the door, "come in and sit down, won't you. I'm sorry I have not been in touch. All I can tell you is that the exorcism has not been successful, and of course it has worried me. I have looked into the local church records for that area and done some other research, but have not found much of relevance. I will be going down to London soon where I will do some more studies and consult with higher authority. That is all I can tell you for now. How are you – you are looking rather strained. I should not worry about it too much if I were you, you can forget the matter and let me handle it from now on."

"But I can't forget it – she comes to me in the night."

"Ah, yes, I see. These things are very unnerving to some people. That is why I suggest you see Dr. Lorenson." He looked at me with some concern, and got up. "I will ring her now and make an appointment for you." He left the room. Ten minutes later he came back in and handed me a card.

"Here is her address and the date and time, it's all arranged."

"I have seen psychiatrists before you know."

"Yes, well that may be. But Dr. Lorenson will probably be more help to you, she specialises in cases such as yours that I pass on to her, and you will find her approach quite different and more understanding."

I was not convinced, but I said, "Well okay, I had better see somebody before I crack up."

I called at the office of Dr. Elizabeth Lorenson, as arranged, and she welcomed me with a smile. I had not known what to expect, but she was young and attractive, and I relaxed a bit.

"Now what is your full name?"

"Paul Thompson."

"Age?"

"29, but I hope you are not going to ask me all those questions I had to answer at the hospital."

"No, I have quite a lot of that information already. But tell me, have you felt a loss of self-esteem lately?"

"I suppose so."

"Have you become more withdrawn into yourself?"

"Well I suppose I have. Who wouldn't when you have seen what I have seen. I have answered all these questions before, but it is not depression and I am quite sure I am not schizophrenic or something."

"What I propose to do is delve into your subconscious. We will arrange a number of exploratory sessions. For now just tell me how you feel."

"Not bad, now I'm with you," I wisecracked.

"Now now, Mr. Thompson. We must take this seriously, Reverend Hughes tells me you have been quite ill."

"Yes, I suppose I have. We could not banish this

spirit I saw and I kept seeing her in my dreams – most disturbing dreams – I felt insecure, there didn't seem to be any solid rational ground to stand on anymore."

"I see – I think if we can find the basis or origin of your fears we will get you back to stability. Try not to worry. Come to see me at 10 a.m. on Tuesdays and Thursdays, starting next Tuesday, a week today."

At the next interview on the following Tuesday she led me into an adjoining room fitted with a couch.

"Try to relax, without feeling afraid, you are safe here – and tell me of these fears you have, slowly and calmly."

I did my best to recall the events, but now I was with her they seemed to have receded into the distance.

"This Sophia may be a figure from your childhood, and you may have had experiences with her which you have repressed into your subconscious."

"I'm sure I have never seen her before."

"No, but the figures and events can become transposed on to other figures. Lie back on the couch and relax. Think back to when you were 4 or 5 years old, relax. Can you see anything, what do you see?"

Her questions went on without revealing much and I grew tired.

Sensing this she said, "Well I will see you on Thursday then. Take care."

Thursday came. I lay on the couch and looked at her. I reached up to take hold of her hand. She automatically resisted, withdrawing her hand, then she put it back. Somehow I felt an attraction – I did not know nor had little hope that she would like me in my condition – but I felt this chemistry between us. The longer our hands clasped the stronger the feeling got. Love is a strange thing, I wonder what it is. exactly. Initially of course it is just the natural attraction of opposites, of positive and negative, of male and female – but there has to be something more, some close comradeship, some feeling of having known her or him before, perhaps from the beginning of time – and then it is certain, inevitable, irrevocable, nothing can part you from the beloved, nothing – nothing on earth that is.

"We must try to concentrate on revealing any childhood fears or bad experiences you have had," she said.

"Must we? Why?"

"To get you back to feeling normal again. I do not mean you are abnormal, there is no such thing in modern psychology. It is not my job to put labels on people, I do not work that way. Nobody is abnormal, but the way in which a person may conceive the events in their life can affect their quality of life. From this standpoint any problems can simply be resolved by reviewing the object or event, or the trauma, and looking at it differently, that is with a positive enabling conception, instead of from a negative perspective, which produces loss of self-esteem and its associated problems."

"But that's not what I want. You know I want you. I love you. With your love I am cured, I need nothing else, only you."

"Patients often fall in love with their doctors, and it would seem with their psychiatrists too."

"You regard me just as a patient then? I've never felt more normal in my life, at this moment, with you. I know my nerves have been shattered, but I assure you I did not dream it up. It was real all right."

"If you saw this, as indeed you say you did, then however it occurred then it is real to you. My job is to calm and remove any phobias you might have. We can achieve this in a number of ways, and I am sure we will be able to find one that will work in your case. I think we should explore your reactions to these events or manifestations and replace them with more positive reactions and strategies that will enable you to regain your self-confidence."

She rambled on while I, only half listening, looked at her, drinking in her beauty. She was fair, almost blonde, aged 27, lovely in every way, and I was nearly 30. Just then the phone rang in the office and she was away for at least fifteen minutes.

"That was John on the phone. Apparently he has been doing some research in London – and he has been telling me a long tale of a legendary figure he thinks might be your apparition. However, I'm afraid I don't understand it all, I'm a plain austere scientist myself," she laughed gaily. "Perhaps he will tell you about it when you see him next." She looked at her watch, "My, the time has flown. I will see you next Tuesday then."

Later on in our relationship she related this phone conversation to me, which apparently went as follows:

"I have discovered some records and an old legend, a story about a Sophia Sancire, which may have some bearing on this apparition of Paul's."

"It's not a figment of his imagination then. I thought he may have read some story in his childhood at a highly

67

impressionable age, which has become repressed in his subconscious ever since."

"No, I'm afraid it is rather more than that, I have also seen this woman. There is an evil power at work here. I did not want to admit it before. I don't think you should revive the memory of this in Paul. There are some things it is best to steer.clear of if you can."

"You surprise me, John! You realise of course that we psychologists have no place for such things as immaterial apparitions in actuality, although they may appear real and be a reality to the persons involved. To scientists all things have evolved in a material universe and have a rational logical explanation."

"Yes, Liz. But we theologians believe there is also an immaterial world, the world of the soul, which is good. But there may also be unquiet spirits trapped in an in-between world, which is where my work comes in. In this case the exorcisms were not successful." He sighed, "However, that's my worry. I just thought I had best let you know what I had discovered about this legend, in case it helps you in your overview of the case, your assessment."

"All right John. Thanks a lot. Bye."

CHAPTER 4

The following Tuesday her attitude towards me seemed to have softened. I think John's phone call had given her a different perspective of me, perhaps I was not paranoid after all, not suffering from a psychological disorder. I was laying on the couch as usual, but she was looking at me differently, hesitating, not talking as much as usual.

"Well, well," I grinned, "You've stopped treating me as a patient."

A slightly embarrassed smile came to her face. "I like your smile. In fact there is quite a lot I like about you."

"I bet there is," she arched her eyebrows provocatively.

I got up, took her hand, and brought her to me. "Let's throw the psychology out of the window, the apparition too, everything – all I want is you." We kissed, a long gentle caressing kiss that lasted forever. From that moment life was a joy, there was only one thing in my head. Yes, I needed Elizabeth, without her I was nothing, with her I possessed the world. And she needed me. She was a woman who wanted to help others, and making psychiatry as her chosen profession was a way of doing this, in much the same way as many an idealistic doctor might subconsciously do. She must have been lonely too, longing for an intimate companionship. I guess I just happened to come along at the right time. We needed each other, and our love blossomed. The sun filled the world with its light, and the green buds were bursting forth on the trees, don't ask me how, that wonderful morning in October. Yes, the world was filled with love, she had given me a reason for living, and I was reprieved – for a time.

In one of my letters to her I wrote:

My darling, my dearest one, you are my life, my light, my love. I live for you and you give life to me, you light up my life with happiness – and I love you. Love is magic, nothing is greater or more powerful. Love is my King, and you are my Princess. I love you with all my heart; and more than anything in this whole wide world I want to marry you, to be yours forever, 'to have and to hold you, to love and to cherish you.' On the day of April 21st I will pledge my life to you. May the magic ef true love be ours.

In this enchanted world of love right triumphed over wrong my heart sang within me. When we danced, with her in my arms, it was as if we were in the clouds, as if we were one, made for each other. When we looked at each other across a table, when we paddled in the sea, when we sat on the beach or the promenade on a summer evening, our hands would meet – and in that simple gesture was a meaning beyond all words, a power to transcend all. I stood her on a pedestal for did I not owe my life to her. She had rescued me from fear, doubt, and despair – although it was not because of any psychological knowledge on her part, but simply because of love.

John sent us a present, but wrote to say he was unable to attend the wedding due to indisposition and commitments. After the wedding we moved down south to live and work in Bristol. Love for her had rescued me from the shadows of the mind, but we had eyes only for each other. I had started work again as an analytical chemist in a small firm of consulting chemists, and with the commitment and responsibility of marriage I applied myself to my work. Within five years I had become second in command to the principal director.

We had been married about three years when Elizabeth received a letter from Father Dawson. It contained a shock John Hughes had committed suicide. He had been mentally ill for a long time. Liz rang Father Dawson up, "Why didn't you tell me?" she asked.

"You lived rather far away and he was being treated by other well-trained medical psychiatrists," replied the priest, "I think he wanted to get well before he saw people again."

"It's such a shock," she said, "what a shame."

We forgot about it, of course, and lived our lives.

We were happy in our marriage, although we had no children. But things gradually change, it is the nature of things. Inwardly I suppose we grew more self-confident, and outwardly more affluent. The combination of these factors somehow led to our not being quite so close together. It's odd but when I look back it was the early days when we had little money that were the happiest. I do not imply that we fell out of love, what I mean is that all things change with time; in the incessant churning of the atoms and molecules of existence vibratory natures change, individual organisms evolve and devolve, whole species adapt, the valleys rise and the mountains are laid low for change is the law of nature.

Ten years were to pass, and I was now 42, and my elder brother who had resided in Old Moston, which was near Chadderton, died. I was uncle to their three children although I had never seen them from being a teenager. Although I was their uncle they were not all that much younger than me. One had disappeared into the army, another had married a rich Jew, I think. However the youngest daughter had had an unhappy marriage and had little money, she lived alone in that area. About six weeks after the funeral I decided to go up and visit her. Elizabeth and I had both been to the funeral of course, but this time I went alone.

I called at the old rectory in Rochdale on the way and had a chat and a cup of tea with Father Dawson, who was now getting on in years and, due for retirement.

"It was such a shock about Reverend Hughes," I said. "I would never have thought it of him, he was so level headed and devoted to his work."

"One can never tell," he mused. "By the way, there is an old diary of his here. I think there are some notes about your case in it, that time when you had some psychological disturbance. I was going to give it to Elizabeth, but I have not seen her since John's death, and I never got around to it. You can take it and give it to her, now that you are here. It would really only be of interest to such as her, I think." It was quite a large diary, one suitable for a scholar with plenty of room for notes. I took the book with me.

I put up at an hotel in Chadderton, a small gloomy affair – the sun never seemed to shine in those leafy streets, the trees cast a permanent shadow. Looking out of the back window I could see the canal – awakening dark memories.

I visited my niece Barbara that day, a fairly gentle creature but with a mind of her own. I enjoyed her company, took her out for a walk and a meal, and made a mental note that I must leave her something in my will. Somehow though I wanted to get back to the hotel to read that diary. Taking off my coat and shoes, and putting on the comfortable pair of slippers that I had brought with me, I sat down in an armchair and settled down to read it. Although it was still only early in the evening it looked as if it might take some time to wade through it, to find any relevant material. The diary was for the year when Elizabeth and I first met, about eleven years ago. Apparently he had not written anything further between that year and his death.

CHAPTER 5

THE DIARY OF JOHN HUGHES

Sept. 17 I went alone on the third night. Paul Thompson was averse to going, it must be affecting him. I must admit I did not sleep so well myself last night. It was lonely, dark and eerie, and she was not banished – for she soon appeared to me, coming very close which unnerved me, and looking at me with unblinking eyes, unfathomable dark eyes – and yet she did not look evil. As I read the incantation she smiled and remained looking at me. The incantation had no effect whatsoever and I became afraid, a power seemed to radiate from her and I knew she was stronger than me – far, far stronger. And then dark images came into my mind, images of worlds within worlds, universes within universes, where I and even all mankind were as nothing. "I am Sophia," she said, and I turned and ran from her.

Sept. 20   At first I was in a kind of stupor, then over the next two days I gradually got back to normal. I have decided that I must go down to the Little Vatican offices in London, study the archives, and learn what else I can do.

Received a phone call from Paul this morning. He sounded upset – have asked him down to see me tomorrow and will put him in touch with Elizabeth.

LONDON visit arranged for Sept. 22–29.

Sept. 23 Visited the archives, housed in the basement of the Church Administration Offices. These offices were once used in the times of the Inquisition, subsequently rebuilt they now serve many administrative functions, one Department of which embraces my own particular employment. I have unearthed the following record:

A Sophia Sancire who had established a convent on the isle of Iona in the sixteenth century was brought before the Inquisitorial Court accused of heresy. The charge was rather vague, and appeared to arise because her Order had become too successful for the comfort of the church authorities. Her words to her persecutors are recorded thus:

"Do I not know thee for what thou art? Self-righteous vindictive men who wish to play with their prey, for you have already pre-judged all who walk through that door. You cannot judge me or gainsay me for you lack mystical wisdom. I know thee and what thou art, but you are not able to know me for I have advanced on high. My will is law, not least in my own convent. For am I not more enlightened than you? Are you not an open book to me? Beware. For if you pronounce me guilty, you pronounce yourselves guilty. Do you not understand this?"

This offended the tribunal. The head of the Court, a Cardinal Vincent, gave his judgement:

"You have disobeyed the Holy See and succumbed to the sin of pride, which is the most abominable in a woman. We also find you guilty of heretical thoughts, therefore it is the judgement of this Court that the Devil shall be driven out of you."

As far as the tribunal was concerned that was the end of the matter, of their involvement, but not for Sophia. She was taken to the cells below to find out over the next few days what was meant by 'the Devil shall be driven out of you' – physical torture in the dungeons of the Inquisition. There existed refined and terrible instruments of torture in those days that have long since been outlawed. When she was finally released it was to learn that she had been ex-communicated by papal decree.

Sept. 24   Today I visited the Rylands library to look through old books and manuscripts of mediaeval legends. One story described a founder of a religious order named Sophia who was an angelic creature inspired by God, who was falsely accused by her enemies. This turned her vengeful and she vowed to establish her own Order in the spiritual world – and then she willed herself to die. She was stated to have a will stronger than that of any human being before or since. Another story quoted her as saying, 'All men will eventually bow down to me, will bend to my will, when I, Sophia, call them. For my will is the law, and in me you shall see your judgement.' There were too old stories of succubi, ensnarers of men's souls, but I do not know if this Sophia is such a being.

There was no record of where she was buried.

Sept. 27   Today I had an interview with my superior. Bishop Matthewson was portly, he enjoyed the good life, and his wine cupboard was well stocked. "Would you like a drink, John? A white Chablis or Madeira, or a sweet Marsala or perhaps a liqueur – Chartreuse, Benedictine?" He settled comfortably in his chair. "Now what can I do for you?" I told him that I had met with an apparition, a manifestation of evil, which the normal ceremony was not strong enough to banish, and I needed access to an exorcism rite of greater efficacy, greater power.

He seemed a bit taken aback. "That sounds like a rather serious proposal. We do not often have cause to open such things in these days. Perhaps I may be able to set your mind at ease."

I gave him the details. He pursed his lips, and poured out more drinks, "Have another, my friend. Now, these things sometimes disappear or resolve themselves. Perhaps if you go there again this apparition will have gone, if not you could try the usual ceremony once more."

I could see that he did not really want to be bothered with it – but I knew she was still there, so I persisted. A frown of irritation passed across his face, but then he smiled and relapsed into his usual relaxed, if slightly pompous manner. Then he looked across at me with a serious expression. "Well, you know John, it will mean opening old archives but I will do that for you, if you really feel it is necessary. But there are two or three factors to be taken into consideration or should I say facets of this situation that I must counsel you about. The first point is that any stronger incantation is not to be taken lightly, for these are serious matters even beyond my ken, for dangerous powers may be unleashed. The greater a weapon one uses against a foe, the greater the weapons they will use in return. Then too I am not at all convinced it is necessary, especially in these more enlightened times – I prefer a quiet life if possible. Of course it is you who are in the field, the front line so to speak, not I – but you will appreciate that all these matters come under my jurisdiction. I am in charge of the records and the archives and the final responsibility rests with me – so you put me in something of a dilemma."

He was silent for a while. "I will tell you what – come and see me tomorrow, after lunch. I should have something for you by then." He got up and ushered me to the door.

Sept. 28   Soon as I walked in, he said, "There must be no publicity, the Department must not be involved in any way, and you must send me an ordered and concise report when your investigation is complete." I could see that he had decided that 'the poor chap' could have what he wanted as long as it did not impinge directly on his own well-ordered life! I agreed, and he handed me a sealed brown parchment envelope, which I am to open privately when I get back home. I rang up Elizabeth to tell her the result of my researches.

Oct. 30   I have now carefully prepared my plan to exorcise this spirit, for I regard myself as a crusader of God, or at least of the Church in a battle against the enemy. I append a translation from the Latin of parts of the rite of exorcism, although I cannot display the whole of the original document publicly.

SOPHIA

THE EXORCISM CEREMONY
ANTIQUUS MANDAMUS ARCANUM
FOR THE ABSOLUTION OF SOULS

In this scroll are inscribed the secret instructions and arcane
rites that should only be used in extremis for they release
spiritual powers that must be reverenced and held in awe.

INJUNCTION

Be it known that I, ———— am ordained as a representative
of the Holy Mother Church in these matters of Life and
Death. In return for divine forgiveness you O Soul in
torment are abjured to depart this earth.

If you do not obey this injunction and art a thing of evil I
condemn you to eternal hellfire.

ABSOLUTION

O lost spirit, if thou be not beyond redemption BE AT
PEACE: You are forgiven and thy sins are absolved.

THE EXPURGATION

Begone from this earth plane to the place prepared for thee
For are not all things ordained by God
So even for thee – rebel no more.

THROW THE HOLY WATER ON THE OBJECT and say:
I COMMAND THEE IN THE NAME OF THE MOST
HIGH

EXEGESIS The authentic words and order must be
preserved
It is unwise to attempt any alteration in this ceremony

Nov. 18. The water went right through her and she still stood there facing me, smiling and at the same time threatening.

"Do you dare to hurl your little spells at me? Are you the witch or am I? You understand nothing, you are little more than nothing – you know that, do you not? For you just flitter about the edge of Life, with no real grasp of what is or what is to be. Do you not know who and what I am?"

As she said this she loomed over me great, dark and terrible, and suddenly ten thousand demons were unleashed in my mind – leering, they rushed about madly, without purpose, imbecilic. I cried out and fell, half swooning, with my hands over my ears and my eyes closed. She left me. I got to my feet, shaking, cold and wet with perspiration. Thank God she has left me, was my only thought.

There was a blank page, then he had written, undated: I would not go there again, for I know I have no power over her. And she comes to me in my dreams in the night.

There were half a dozen blank pages, then there was the following, again undated: In the nights that have followed I have had little sleep, waking or sleeping the thoughts and dreams oppress me. Every day, every night jumbled thoughts come to my mind that I cannot resolve. I tremble at every recollection of her. I will put these thoughts down – to try to make sense of them.

Rites have no power over her.

She is more mystically evolved than we are.

Compared with the wisdom and knowledge she

possesses I am an empty shell, compared with her power I am insignificant, nothing. I am impotent against her.

My religion is impotent against her, it has let me down, it has been found wanting. Perhaps she is greater than our religion, her great power once good now turned to evil. Or is it we that are evil? Not her! Surely that is not possible? Not her! Not her!

And have I not seen her somewhere before – a long time ago, a long, long time ago.

I know my mind is crumbling, but what can I do. I am ashamed to let Elizabeth know about all this. Has not my religion let me down and failed me – I have nowhere else to turn. I begin to feel now that my whole life has been a failure. Who am I, what am I? Nothing. She is right.

There is no defence against her.

I have been referred to a psychiatrist by the doctor – but they do not know her, they have not seen her.

There is no escape.

Here the diary ended.

CHAPTER 6

Poor John. My sympathies went out to him, for had I not myself been through it. But I had been fortunate, Elizabeth had rescued me. The danger had gone from me – I was now self-confident and above such things. And perhaps also John had felt it more because of his religious beliefs.

Thus I mused, and it must have been nearly two in the morning when I had finished reading and finally retired. I was overtired, and in a strange bed and surroundings. Without Elizabeth to support me, my mind became disturbed. Lying in bed I dreamed fitfully and I sensed Sophia calling me. The moment she appeared in my mind the delusion that I had the strength to resist her was immediately dispelled. That last dream was a nightmare that seemed to last all night, as I tossed and turned in a turmoil.

"Can your Elizabeth rival me now? Does she have my power? Can she give you as much sensuality as this?" She threw off her cloak and an overwhelming wave of lust and depravity poured over me. I threw myself on her. "Yes, give yourself to me," she whispered, "for I have waited for you."

There was a blackness about her, wherein I had a glimpse of serpents writhing and flickering, and in that blackness I seemed to sense that there were other shadowy forms in bestial contortions.

"But what of these others?" I said.

"Forget about them, do not concern yourself with these others, they have their own desires. They are all satisfied, until they become sated, surfeited. Do not worry about these others – it is what you desire, whatever you desire shall come into being. Can you understand this?"

"I think I do," I replied.

I think I fell asleep. Then the nightmare resumed. She came close to me, very close, and wrapped her black habit about me, underneath it we lay naked in an intimacy so great that it was sheer ecstasy, then unendurable, and in the dream I suffocated and died – but did not mind.

Later she appeared to me again, she was smiling with an innocent radiance, almost holy. She was not stained in any way. I suddenly realised she was pure and holy – and it shocked me. For it was me who had wanted to defile her, it was in me where the evil lay, it was all inside me. I did not know what to say or do. Everything seemed to come to a stop, frozen, and all that existed was a sense of horror.

"Oh, Sophia, what have I done to thee in my ignorance?"

"You will come to me tomorrow," she said, "by the canal where we first met, for it is there that I must claim your soul. For there is no escape."

When I awoke I was in a deadly calm. There is no

escape from the sins of the past, even those committed in thought only, I know it now. So I have written this last epistle, as a warning. There is only one thing, one hope, that can keep the shadows at bay, and that is love. But always be careful to whom you entrust that love. Perhaps in spite of all that I have written you think you could gainsay her – but then you have not yet met Sophia.

★★★

I was quite calm and clear-headed as I made my way slowly along the deserted canal path. She was waiting for me. Her power made you tremble with fear. And yet it was not evil in itself, it was pure and strong. It was its very strength that dismayed you.

She had no wish to harm me. There was no evil in her at all. Pure and innocent! But that is what attracts me, what maddens me with desire. It wells up in me, an uncontrollable urge to ravish her until she can stand no more. Well, that is what sex is like, is it not? Admittedly there was no love in this, for my only desire was to defile her – why I did not know. I think it was because of her essential purity, the purity that was hidden in her power, a purity, a perfection, a deep-rooted power that I could not attain to. It may also have been because I realised she was a danger to me.

And a strange horrible thought now occurs to me for a fleeting moment – was I one of those who had condemned her? In that Court, a long long time ago. I could restrain myself no longer and threw myself upon her, even though I knew that I would not be returning from there – not into the sane and living world.

I will hold a mirror up unto thy soul
That you may be judged
For I am SOPHIA.

BACK FROM THE DEAD

"It is really pleasant here, unhurried and peaceful. Do you like it, darling?"

"Yes dear, of course I do." Helen was a most undemanding creature, she had endured sadness and tragedy early in life and was now content just to be with him and enjoy the little pleasures in life. He knew he was lucky to have her. They had been on most of the organised trips, up onto the foothills of the Balkan mountains and a river cruise along the Danube and were taking the last two days of their holiday restfully, sat in the hotel grounds. It was three in the afternoon; the sun was shining in an azure blue sky.

"Let's go for a little walk in the country," he said. The part of Bulgaria they were located in, a little inland from Vama, was rural and unspoilt. The green of the undulating pastures seemed brighter and cleaner than back home, enhanced by the little yellow flowers that dotted them here and there. The hills and slopes were a little taxing however and they realised they had best not venture too far or they would be late for the evening meal. Returning by a different route they passed a cemetery on a hillside to the north-east of the town. It was five o'clock, and Harry led the way across a comer of the cemetery to get to a lane leading back to the hotel. A figure suddenly appeared behind one of the gravestones and startled him. Feeling nervous he positioned Helen on his right side, furthest away from the figure.

"Good afternoon," he said, and they hurried away. For some reason he had been afraid to look directly at the man. "Have you had a nice day?" inquired the maitre d'hotel as they entered.

"Yes, thank you. We came back by a cemetery though and saw a strange-looking man there."

"He does appear there sometimes, and then it is best to keep away for he is an evil man."

"Why don't you inform the police?"

"That would be of no avail, my dear sir. It is not a living man, you understand, but a long dead relative of one of the villagers. A wicked man of a violent temper, he was a man to be shunned."

Harry had smiled at this. Rather naive and superstitious these people, he had thought at the time. But back home he began to think about the matter more seriously. Was there a psychic or spiritual reality or did only the physical universe exist? David, who was an engineer, although having a serious practical inclination, was open-minded.

"I don't think scientists know everything by any means. In fact they now think all this vast universe came into being from nothing!"

"At the big bang, you mean."

"Before the big bang there was nothing, or nothing that we could imagine in physical terms. Then by chance random quantum fluctuation a bubble opened into time and space. So there could be things outside the bubble that are not physical and outside of time and space – but what they are I don't think we can know, so it doesn't matter or concern us."

"From a philosophical point of view, David, we cannot really know what actually exists, only that which appears real to us."

"How do you mean?"

"We do not know what things are like in actuality. We just sense the vibrations of things through our five senses, and those senses form a picture in our minds that we adapt to our physical existence. There is no proof the physical universe exists, at least as it appears to us, indeed some philosophers including Shakespeare have proposed that we are living inside a dream."

"It's certainly a complicated subject. What made you bring this up?"

"Well when I was on holiday in Bulgaria recently I think, although I'm not sure of course, I think I saw a ghost."

"You are joking!"

"No I'm not, and our little discussion has made me see that it is possible. Of course the dead don't rise up and walk, but let us suppose for the moment that we do have a soul as some religions claim, then at death the soul, being nonphysical and untramelled by time and space, departs into the spiritual realm. But a very evil soul could remain chained to its physical body, at least for a time, by its past thoughts and deeds, or to the environment in which it lived – it would be imprisoned in the mental world which it had created for itself. Now if that is the case, then even in this country, although we pride ourselves on our advancement, there must be some similar evil spirits, trapped on this plane as it were. If only we could fmd one such being, to prove things one way or the other."

David laughed. "You would probably have to visit every cemetery in Britain, and even then you may not be there at the right moment."

"That's the problem, but it would explain why there have been so few contacts with ghosts or spirits. The first thing we should do is to get some lists of suitable sites made out and keep records. Too much for one man of course, even over a lifetime. How about helping me in your spare time?"

"It's a sheer impossibility, Harry."

"Not if we get a group together and systematically comb the country. It could still take a lifetime, but just think it could give us the answer to many philosophical questions, not to mention alter scientific thinking. Just help me in your spare time, Dave, that's all I ask."

"Okay, anything for you, my friend."

So Harry began his endeavour, utilising all the spare hours he could grab, often standing alone in dark creepy cemeteries. Helen did her best to deter him, fearing some harm might befall him. He advertised in a local newspaper for 'ghost hunters', and eventually they had formed a group of ten to pursue their interest. They met at David's home every so often to plan their visits and make any reports. Besides David and himself the other members of the group were a pretty varied set of characters, and included

RALPH – a rather bigoted chap who lacked tolerance, everything was black or white to him; he denounced al1 transgressors of the law, regarding himself as good and perfect.

STEVE – who enjoyed the battles of life, and was willing to have a go at anything.

KEN – he was in it for a laugh, and did not take life seriously.

DENBY – a somewhat timid sort, who didn't look as if he would say 'boo' to a goose, never mind a ghost!

CHARLES – a serious scientist, his only aim was to debunk anything of a supernatural nature.

Harry of course was the philosopher type striving to fathom what was real and permanent. And then there was David, serious, intelligent, an engineering background, but open minded and fair. As the years passed without success the other three hunters had gradually dropped out.

At one of their meetings Ralph said, "It's a bit like looking for a needle in a haystack, isn't it?"

"Almost impossible, I said so at the beginning," put in David.

"I agree we are not getting very far," said Harry, "so I have a new plan to propose. Instead of all this travelling, we will advertise for people to send us 'sightings'. Then we will just go and investigate those. I will ring you up to give you the details. During the periods when we have no reports to follow up I hope you will take in some of the places still on our lists as per usual."

Many of the sightings were either false or were to prove fruitless, and some were from cranks. Time passed, and to Harry it was all very disappointing. David was getting fed up at the lack of success. Steve was not too put out; ebullient as ever, he still found it exciting. Ken – well nothing was very serious to him, and Denby did not disclose his real feelings. Ralph was angry and frustrated, he had nothing or no one to attack. Charles had never believed in it, and he would carry on simply to show anybody and everybody that science was the only true God. After seven years Harry was on the point of giving up when one day, shortly after he had re-inserted the advertisement in the paper, he received an odd phone call.

"It happened some years back actually," said the voice, "so when I first saw your advert I didn't reply because I thought it was too late in the day. But seeing your ad again recently brought it back so vividly to my mind that I feel I must get it off my chest. Some years ago when I was courting I was sat in the car with my girl petting and canoodling. I was parked outside this cemetery which had a three foot wall with iron railings on top and the ground was raised up inside I think. Anyway I was on the offside, and my face was buried in my fiancée's neck and hair when out of the corner of my eye I saw this demon, leaning over us as it seemed. It was inside the railings but it was so evil, terrifying and menacing that it seemed to be almost in the car. I started the car quick and hared it away like a bat from hell and I have never been near the place since."

Harry was suddenly all attention, and excited: "What was it like?"

"After all this time I couldn't tell you, nor would I want to recollect it and tell you – I think it was the Devil himself."

"Where was it?"

"It is called Phillips Park cemetery in an area of Manchester known as Bradford. A very old and very large cemetery, dark and forbidding in parts. The land to the south, and also for a good way to the east and southwest, is desolate and derelict, lying in a vale or hollow that is spanned by a large seven-arched railway viaduct. To the north is the Miles Platting area of Manchester, to the south the industrial areas of Clayton and Beswick."

"Do you recall the time?"

"It would be about half twelve at night."

"But you have not seen it since?"

"I would never go there again, not for a million pounds. Just the faint recollection of it brings a shiver to my spine."

Harry contacted the remaining group members, and then booked rooms at the Portland hotel in the centre of Manchester.

Charles objected, "But wasn't this occurrence some years ago?"

"True, it may not be there now. On the other hand if my theories are correct they are chained to this earth plane perhaps for centuries or until they are at last able to change – repent would be the theological expression – but of course I may be wrong."

"Alright, I will come, but you know my views and I for one don't expect we will see anything."

Having all assembled at the hotel Hany spoke to the

group and asked, "Shall we go tonight and get it over with, or would you like to rest up and go tomorrow?"

Ken was all for a nightclub and a drink, but as everyone else did not particularly want to hang around he agreed to fall in with the majority.

"I will order taxis for eleven o'clock. So you have a couple of hours yet in which to enjoy yourself, Ken. I will probably see the rest of you in the bar before we leave."

They arrived at the cemetery about half eleven. The taxi drivers looked suspiciously at them and drove off. "The gates are locked," said David.

"Now what do we do?" said Denby, "those gates must be at least twelve feet high."

"We will try walking round the side, we should be able to find a gap of sorts in a big place like this," suggested Steve. They walked to the left; after a hundred and fifty yards the wall turned south and about two hundred yards further along this side the iron railings were gone and parts of the wall had either crumbled or fallen down, and they passed inside.

"Where did he say he saw it?" asked Charles.

"I'm not all that sure," answered Harry. "It was most likely near the front where the roads are, near the front gates towards the eastern side. He was parked on a road, but it is unlikely to have been the main road – that runs along the west side."

They made their way back to near the main gates, then along the inner side of the wall for about eighty yards to the east. Here they stopped and hid themselves down behind the headstones – they were all pretty experienced at it by this time – and began to settle down and relax. Without warning the apparition appeared as if from nowhere, leering, and looming menacingly over them, absolutely evil, and ejaculating incessantly. They were startled and terrified out of their wits. The sheer lust and sexual depravity of the thing shocked the senses and numbed the mind.

It had been their plan to surround the ghost and hope their combined number and purpose could oppose and somehow overpower it, whilst they made their notes and observations, but that plan was shattered and swept away in this sudden onslaught of obscenity, and the assault upon their minds of this evil almost beyond comprehension.

The demon, the apparition, or whatever it was, seemed to rear up at them and they recoiled in horror and fled from its overpowering evil in sheer panic. To describe the fear that coursed through them is impossible to convey in words. They fled in different directions, anywhere, anyhow, to get away from it, and escape over the wall. Outside they somehow managed to find each other and dashed towards a phone box, unable to speak. Harry forced his fingers and voice to work sufficiently to call the taxi firm, before reaction set in. Denby was scared out of his wits. As they clambered into the taxis only Steve managed to utter, "Let's get away from here."

In the hotel next morning they recalled the events of the preceding night. "Was that thing alive? It looked real and alive, but absolutely hideous and frightening, from another world," said David.

"It looked more like a skeleton to me, under

mouldering clothes, but it was alive alright, capering about, demonic," Ralph put in. Denby and Ken were still stunned and silent. Charles too was shocked by the experience: "But it may be some maniac who inhabits the place for self-gratification and for sexual perversities. You do get some people like that," he appealed to them, trying to cling on to his shaken beliefs.

"That was no ordinary human," said Harry, "how could it keep ejaculating like that? And why did we run – because we knew it wasn't human, and the fact that we each saw it in slightly different ways shows that it was a spirit entity, and not physical."

Of the group he alone seemed cheerful, for inside he felt a kind of satisfaction. "Well we have proved it at last," he said. "That's all I wanted."

"Yes, but it's absolutely bestial and filled with sexual depravity, shouldn't we do something about it?" said Ralph.

"I think it is best to leave it alone, that is what they advised me in Bulgaria, and I think they are right. You cannot destroy these things because they are spirits." Ralph however was unwilling to let the matter rest. He was driven by a desire to rid the earth of this hateful thing and tried to persuade them to go with him.

"Come on, Steve, let's destroy it. How about you, Ken?" But there was no laughter now on Ken's face. "You will never get me to go there again."

Denby at last found his voice, "Nor me, it was a satyr from hell if there ever was one. Its legs looked like the hind legs of a goat." Charles also demurred. If it was a crank then it did not concern him, he was neither vindictive nor intolerant. However deep down he now knew, as the others did, that this was no human they had seen, for it had struck him with an overwhelming fear, a power of evil that had frozen him with inertia, motionless and dumb, until blind panic motivated his limbs into action. And he wanted no part of it for they could not harm it for it had no physical substance.

Only Steve finally agreed to accompany Ralph on another expedition to the cemetery to confront the object.

"What weapons do you propose to take?" inquired Harry. "Something not too obvious, how about a pickaxe and spades, as if we are workmen," said Ralph.

A few days later reading the paper one morning Harry suddenly exclaimed to his wife, "I told them to leave well alone. There is nothing you can do against them."

"What's that?" his wife asked.

"I was just reading this article in the newspaper. Two men were found brutally murdered in a cemetery in Manchester, the head of one was almost severed from the body by a spade, and the other one was found with a pickaxe through his chest. I was talking to them only last week, they were in our group."

"How awful. I knew no good would come of it all, promise me you will stop these psychic investigations of yours."

"I've achieved what I set out to do. I'm keeping well clear of such things from now on, darling," he assured her.

AHRIMAN

He had started going into the city centre to the big library with his elder brother. It was a treasure house to him with thousands upon thousands of weird and wonderful books to be discovered on every subject under the sun. And it was some time later that he found the alcove devoted to metaphysical studies, and ever afterwards he found himself drawn there. Eventually he began to take out on loan the half dozen or so books that dealt with occultism and the black arts. One book in particular he pored over for many months, a strange book, written by one Magister Eliphas Levi. At first he was simply interested and fascinated by the subject. Later, in his twenties, it was power over others that he unconsciously sought.

Late in the night when the rest of the family were asleep he would creep downstairs and lay out the black cloth, the mirror, and the candles on the bureau – this was his altar. Opening the book he would study and try to discern its hidden messages and procedures, that was like a misted window into the great mysterious world of unseen spirits and powers, and the wisdom possessed by only the few earnest aspirants – but this occult knowledge was heavily veiled. It was a secret world, occult, not open to the idly curious, for such pearls were not to be indiscriminately cast before swine. Why these pearls seemed to be predominantly black, not white, worried him sometimes. The books were not explicit as to the aims and purpose of these practises, and this too disturbed him a little. He desired to delve into hidden teachings and mysteries but he would have preferred white magic to black and these books seemed to be inclined to the latter, however as they were the only ones available to him they would have to do. There was another drawback; although the subject interested him greatly and he understood its theory there appeared to be little in the way of practical instruction, and he gained the impression that one had to apply oneself in a long period of supplication, doing one's own experiments, until one released the powers from beyond – or was 'accepted'. He was not sure what these powers would then do or how he would control them.

As it transpired he did not advance that far in his studies before other natural forces and interests intervened and, at the age of twenty-five, he married Katrina. His love for Katrina blotted out all other thoughts from his mind, to him she shone with an open almost innocent joy and radiance, so different from his own tense tormented interior, and he instinctively knew he was indeed fortunate to have her. It was only after they had been married ten years or so that the larger perplexing questions of existence began to interest and obsess him again. What was life and death? Why were we here? One question in particular perturbed him – there was no reason to presuppose that life forms on the earth plane were the only entities in the universe. Are there then powers in the universe or on other planes apart from human powers?

He returned to his study of occultism in more earnest. The symbols and signs were important for they expressed the ideas succinctly, and had perhaps also an hidden power. The rites and procedures must be in the correct order, that is have systematic purpose. But of most importance was the language to be used, an ancient Persian language. But then again, it was not so much the language as the tongue, it was the sounds that held the key. Many people have found this part of the ritual hard to grasp, and have even derided it – to their peril, but you see it is THE VIBRATIONS. And here I must insert a note of caution: The sounds of EHM and MA should not be used for they neutralise the power of BA and THOTH.

From his studies and referring to his notes the steps to be taken seemed to be as follows:

1. To establish an altar, a consecrated secret sanctum, a place where the planes could meet, and THE BEINGS manifest.
2. To be in possession of the secret words of command, the symbols and signs.
3. To arrange all these things in procedural order, and perform the proper rites.

It was a long time before he at last divined that he had the proper rites in his possession and was ready to proceed. He arranged an altar in his study. His wife rarely visited him there, and he could easily hide all the paraphernalia in his desk before opening the door. However, his attempts seemed to meet with little success and growing tired, he closed his eyes and half-dozed in his chair. Then he felt a presence, some kind of power or energy, near him and opening his eyes saw a dark indeterminate shape.

The Being slowly appeared, as if it was forming itself out of the molecules of the air. It was huge, black, pulsating with an evil energy. "I will make myself known to you," it said, "by this sign you will know me," and it thrust forward its massive head, and on its forehead appeared a circle, inside which a triangle pointed upwards, and inside the triangle two serpents writhed in an endless attempt to swallow each other up by their tails.

"My name is AHRIMAN. If you come to us and join us in our Order I will reward you with a little of my great power."

Black cobwebs seemed to permeate into his brain. "You will soon be ready for us," it said, and departed.

It had been terrifying, so close to that darkness, yet now he began to feel exhilarated. This was the way, to be more than human perhaps, for had it not said it would give him some of its power. At night he was drawn inexorably to his altar, to try to make contact with that dark satanic horror again. Itr was like a drug, filling him with both fear and ecstasy. And the second visitation came.

Seated at his altar he recalled the instructions:

When the vibrations are right the candle flames will enlarge and tremble. A darkness will evolve between them. Do not look at it or be afraid but concentrate on the candle flames. Let the blackness cover you, and you will be absorbed into its life.

A thrill of horror ran through him and his gaze was drawn to the dark thing pulsating and taking shape and form before him. He sensed it was evil, an evil beyond comprehension that would take him for its own. He got up and backed away. The door handle rattled and he turned towards it. He had locked the door, but his wife must have obtained the spare key. She came in – and saw his face.

"What is it, Harry? What are you doing?"

"It's alright. I will explain later, you must go."

She walked past him, looking at the altar and the burning candles.

Then she sensed the blackness, and backed away.

"I will tell you about it later," he said, and ushered her out. He sat down rattled. The thing was still there but it had ceased its growth and was still. He got hold of his notes hurriedly and ran through the instructions for bringing the manifestation to an end. And then it spoke, the voice coming into his mind, commanding, "When you come to me again you must bring her too, for I desire her."

"She will not come, she is not like us." The picture of her innocence and. beauty that he carried in his heart came before his mind.

"I know what you mean. It is those I desire most of

all Bring her to me, and we shall see. And I will reward you."

His mouth was dry and something felt stuck in his throat. He should not get his wife involved in this. But he was hooked on its very horror, caught in a web of evil. He forced the words out. "Come with me tonight in my study, and I will show you the experiments that I have been doing."

"If you want me to, darling. You know I will do anything for you."

He immediately regretted his words – but now it was done.

Later that night he said, "I've been thinking. You had best not come, you might not like it."

"But I want to come now, to see what you have been up to."

Calm and strong inside, she pictured herself as his guiding hand and protector.

Open and receptive, and completely unsuspecting, Ahriman sucked her mind and soul away, and her body fell lifeless before him. He heard her last despairing call to him, and he buried his head in his arms.

"Do not be too concerned. She is with us now."

But he was horrified. What had he done? What evil madness was this? He ran from the room and called for a doctor, but he knew she was dead. A heart attack, perhaps induced by a sudden shock was the medic's verdict, but as she was young and previously healthy a post mortem was desirable.

Her death did not seem to affect him unduly at the time, for he was still absorbed in his arcane pursuits, and

Ahriman had rewarded him it seemed. He exulted for a while in the power given him. He found he had some control over the elements, the vibratory conditions of the air. Minds weaker than his own were his to bend to his will, to subvert, to ensnare, to seduce. But then he began to long for his wife, and the feeling of love – the giving and receiving of love – but he knew she was gone for ever, even as he petitioned Ahriman.

"I want you to give my wife back to me, if that is possible."

"But you have given her to us, there is no going back. You cannot find her again unless you come to our plane, perhaps at your death. But why wait, give yourself to us now, mind and soul, and you can have immortality in our world. Then they did not possess him completely yet." There was a deep inner part of him that still resisted, and had a power of its own. If he did not succumb to their evil he might still retain his own soul. But what of his wife, they had taken her and he was guilty, guilty of sacrificing the greatest possession he had known or could ever know – Love. Could he now sacrifice his own soul to find her again? Had he the courage? And would it not probably be in vain anyway – both of them lost forever in the grip of terrible evil? Why had he delved into these things? Why had he wanted power? Why had he thrown love away? Why, why, why?

"Show me my wife," he demanded. "What have you done with her?"

"We cannot, for even we are subject to the Law."

"What are these laws, and who made them?"

The power in Ahriman faltered and shrank for a moment, but then flared out in wicked belligerence.

"There are other powers – but they as well as we must all obey the laws set in the beginning of creation. They dare not interfere with us, we are supreme in our own domain."

"But then there are forces greater than you – forces for good."

"It is too late for you to go back. Yield to the darkness, let yourself be absorbed into us."

He was suddenly filled with a loathing for Ahriman, he wanted to smash the altar and destroy the books, but he knew he had no strength against the overwhelming evil, and Ahriman cried, "If you go, you will never see your wife again."

His will wavered. He knew there was no going back without her, that he would not be whole without her, would not be accepted back without her. For he now knew the laws. No one can gainsay the Law, although they might think so for a time, the laws set in the beginning of time, immutable. He was a part of her and she a part of him.

He surrendered himself to the darkness, and felt it creep insidiously into his every cell and fibre of his being. "Forgive me," he said, but it was to Katrina and his own soul that he spoke.

Ahriman was not listening, but gloating. "Now I have you in my power – and you are a part of me."

ENCOUNTERS WITH SOPHIA

(i)

He was in a quiet mood of sadness and reverie as he read the inscriptions on the tombs. Words that spoke of loss, at the death of a parent, a spouse, or saddest of all a young daughter, so it was a sudden jolt when he almost bumped into the woman who appeared to have come from nowhere, dressed in black, composed and serene. He admired and was attracted by her poise and tranquility. He was always a bit tense and agitated himself and wished he could be like that. Single and twenty five he was also in need of a girl to love him, although he did not realise this consciously at the time. "Hello," he said, but the woman made no reply. He did not give in too easily: "Not bad for the time of year. Oh, I'm sorry, you may have someone buried here," he trailed off rather lamely.

"No, perhaps I can help you," she smiled questioningly, and he looked into eyes of such depth and clarity, such power and wisdom, that he was abashed and stepped back involuntarily. He sensed that she had a power and strength much greater than his own.

"Do not be afraid. What do you seek in life?"

He was not sure if he actually heard her words, or they just came into his mind. He approached closer to her again, "I seek a beautiful girl like you," and he tried to take her hand, but she withdrew it. Pictures came into his mind, pictures of tender love, with a girl in his arms, her face upheld to his, a face of trust and hope, but a face that somehow became sad and distorted as he framed it in his hands.

"You must learn patience," she said, as she left him.

He was twenty-eight when he met Hazel at a dance, at a small social club where she was a volunteer helper. Medium blonde with bluey-green eyes. They danced, and as he held her in his arms and their eyes met he realised he was seeing that same vision he had seen in his mind three years earlier. He sensed that somehow fate was involved, although he had never believed in such a thing before.

"You know, I have seen you before, in my dreams," he said.

"Well that's a nice line anyway," she replied.

From the first moment they seemed meant for each other, and after a whirlwind courtship embarked on married life together.

Sometimes he was impatient, snappy, and moody. Sometimes he kicked the dog, slammed the door and stormed out; sometimes he was jealous and angry. He did not want to do any of these things, he loved her, but it was the flaws in his nature. After all, are we not all a mixture of good and bad, of strengths and weaknesses, and isn't it so very difficult to change one's spots? She bore it all with patience and stoicism. Gradually but very slowly he came to comprehend some of his faults.

It was much later in life, during one of his periods of contemplation, that musing on whether in some afterlife his sins would be forgiven he remembered the woman in the cemetery. Thinking about her, she came to him. She was still robed in black, but a golden halo about her radiated supreme power and wisdom.

"Thank you for giving me Hazel," he said, without quite knowing why. "I know now that I didn't really deserve her. Can you forgive me?"

She smiled at him. "You have travelled a little on the Path. But we must all pay our debts eventually, it is the law of Karma."

"I once hoped that you would love me."

"You know that cannot be. But one day perhaps you will come to me, and love me."

"Who are you?"

"I am Sophia."

(ii)

She stood directly in my path facing me, with – forgive the pun, quite unintended I assure you – the ghost of a smile upon her face. I say pun because I sensed even then that she was a ghost or spirit, ordinary people do not suddenly appear in front of you from nowhere, nor do they have a kind of halo from which waves of energy seemed to emanate, like radiations from the sun. I was a brash enough laddie and did not back away from anything, not usually that is, but I backed away from her alright. Then I turned and ran. I went home a different way, and on getting home I berated myself for my cowardly panic, then I shrugged the incident off and forgot about it as it faded from memory. After all, I was only twelve days old at the time and had plenty of other things to think about. On odd occasions I would sometimes wonder who she was and why it had happened to me, but I was twenty six by the time I saw her again. But first perhaps I should tell you a bit about myself.

My name is Peter Wilson, in structural design for an engineering firm. My wife keeps me pretty busy putting up the usual shelves and wall cabinets, French windows in the lounge, and even building the garage – well you name it – but I really prefer to be outdoors playing cricket or bowls. Now all this seems fairly ordinary stuff so why did she pick on me? By this time I had matured a bit, had stopped chasing women, and had married and settled down, and I think I am quite level-headed.

Well I think so, let's put it that way. Emotionally mature – well we all have illusions about ourselves! Now I come to think of it perhaps there is something a little odd about me – I don't swear or join in ribald jokes very much, a bit odd in these days, but I just don't like it, it's not me. But don't get me wrong, I am no fuddy duddy, I don't mind other people doing their thing, and believe in live and let live, and I've sown my share of wild oats when I was young! Anyway I was out rambling with one of the county groups one Sunday and we stopped for our lunch – it was the usual thing to take a flask and sandwiches – outside this small village church. After lunch and before we set off again I took a walk around the churchyard reading the epitaphs on the headstones, one of my odd interests. As I got to a quiet corner away from everybody she was there standing before me. Well this time I could not very well run without seeming to show myself up in front of everybody, so I stood my ground. Her eyes were unblinking, and pierced into me as if she saw inside me, into my soul. She seemed strong and powerful, and yet she was small, slender, feminine.

"I am Sophia," she said, without speaking.

"Hello," I managed to mumble, as I edged back towards the side of the church where my fellow ramblers were. I kept quiet about the incident, they would only have laughed at me. What did it mean? What did she want? Whence came her power? How did she speak? All these puzzling thoughts and questions only came to me later as I was on my way home. Later that night I dreamt about her – and she came into my mind.

"I appear to many, but they do not know me for they are not yet ready. I will point your way to the future, if you do not fear, and have faith in me."

"I don't know," I said, "I've got my wife to look after, and my job, why me, I'm not ready." I warded her off and tried to dismiss her from my mind. But before she left me she said, "Perhaps not yet, Peter. You must find the path. When you have travelled some way along that path you will meet me again. In the meantime listen not to the deceivers for they err but know it not." I never saw her again.

Not that is till this last week, which brought those previous incidents back to me from the distant past, and I have written them down. That time in the churchyard must be all of thirty years ago now, and a lot of water has flowed under the bridge since then. I never expected to see her again for I knew she was far beyond me, I'm only an average kind of guy really, maybe less than average. My wife had died, the children gone, I was alone, but I still occupied myself with one or two hobbies. I had more time to meditate however, and maybe that was it. Sat dozing in my chair late one night she came to me, into my mind at first, but then she seemed to be opposite me, looking at me with those eyes that had unfathomable depths in them. Something made me speak:

"I am sorry, Sophia, I was never really clever enough to travel far on that path."

"You do not need to be clever or intellectual, that is not the way of it," came her reply, but she did not speak. It was a telepathic thought I now realised.

"Who are you?"

"I am Sophia, guardian of the flame of Light, knowledge and wisdom."

"But why did you come to me, what can I do, and you must know that I am afraid of you."

"Yes, Peter, I know. And if you would know me you must leave the world of the outer self, the ego, the false world of illusion." There was a sadness in her voice. "Some day you will love me, perhaps a day not far off you will come to me and embrace me, and in return you will receive my power."

"Some day," I said, "but it might take me a million years, are we not all governed by our genes?"

"The worlds of the mind and soul are governed by the laws of the mind and soul, above and beyond the cells of the physical world. Just one second is required, one moment in time. Do not mistake me, the physical world is also divine in its essence, but it is subservient to the centre."

"Where does your power come from, Sophia?"

"You will know when the time comes. Then it will not overwhelm and disconcert you as it does now."

I bowed my head before her, and attempted to kiss her feet, and she disappeared.

EPILOGUE

Now from these tales, some of which actually happened (apart that is from one of the endings, which was contrived in order to provide a suitable dramatic conclusion to the story), let us see what we have established about 'ghosts'.

1. They do exist, although not perhaps as they have been depicted by some. They are not weird shapes under a white sheet, nor can they throw things about physically – although they may be able to do so psychically.

2. They are unlikely to be able to harm you physically or violently, although some of the most evil can come very close to doing that. They are more likely to harm you mentally by the instillation of fear. If you are afraid it encourages them, because the resulting interactive vibrations facilitate their manifestation, that is their appearing to you.

3. Most of them are indeed evil – this is because they are tied by their deeds in their previous life to their bodies, whereas the proper abode of souls is elsewhere. There are also some souls of great

spiritual development who will come to the earth plane for specific purposes.

4. They do not actually speak with vocal chords but by telepathic thoughts.

5. Fortunately for us meetings with ghosts are a rare occurrence and there are at least three reasons for this:

   i) The vast majority of departed souls exist on another plane and are unable to make any contact with the physical plane.

   ii) Those that are still on the earth plane, the evil ones, are tied to their bodies or to a particular place. It is probably as well to avoid deserted cemeteries especially during the small hours of the night. We do not yet fully understand these strings of attachment.

   iii) Most of us are too wrapped up in the material affairs of this world to come into contact with ethereal or psychic forces.

6. Except as regards the stricture of tenet 5(ii) most spirits seem little affected by time and space, the Great Ones not at all.

7. They usually appear to us in the same form they had in their last or previous existence.

8. There is no way whatsoever that we can harm them,

and it is this very fact that can cause us so much fear.

9. As far as 'ordinary' ghosts are concerned they can probably see and hear but it is like an overall psychic sense, not separate senses as we have. They have some sense of touch as well, I think, but they cannot pick things up – that is another common misconception – for they would pass right through the object or the object pass through their hand, one or the other. However, it is a strange and complex subject, even for us mortals, for it is all to do with vibrations. It may be hard to grasp, if you will pardon the pun, but when we touch an object we do not really touch and feel the actual object itself but, as with the other senses, we merely sense the vibrations radiated by the object.

10. They cannot think in the same way that we can, for they have no physical brain, they are thus frustrated and are themselves haunted by a terrible feeling of emptiness.

11. There is another kind of ghost besides the ones mentioned above, but these would not usually be described as ghosts. They are entities, evil powers. It is fortunate indeed that contact with these is extremely rare, for they are terrible to behold, with a power rivaling the Great Ones. A mere mortal would have no chance against them, once in their clutches there is no escape, only eternal despair and longing for the restoration of one's soul.

12. Who are the Great Ones?

Soraya is such a being, and I believe there are many others, but I do not know them for I have not travelled very far on the path. Any one individual would only ever encounter one of them during the course of a lifetime.

Most of us never meet them, not in our present state or stage of development. And what of Sophia? She is something of an enigma, for when I first became acquainted with the narrative of Sophia she seemed to be a self appointed arbiter of karmic retribution, but subsequent fragments revealed in the tales 'Encounters with Sophia' show marked similarities to the role of Soraya, who appeared to me in dreams, and I now believe she also belongs to the order of the Great Ones, although she is perhaps closer to our earth plane. Sometimes they may appear simply to give us a subtle warning, or a prompt to quicken the 'life within' – before it is too late.

What is this mysterious Path? It is not mysterious at all, there are a million paths, and we each follow our own, but eventually the paths begin to merge and so become fewer, especially as they ascend to the mountain top, and it is up here that we may meet one of the Great Ones who will guide us on the greater Path to the summit – to Oneness with the Divine.

All I can say is that Sophia has appeared to some people as is shown in these stories. and I know that Soraya appeared to me albeit only in brief dreams, but in those moments many things were revealed. Just for a moment. And I have often imagined how wonderful it would be if she remained with someone for always. For she revealed to me secrets of heaven and hell, and the greater Path was laid out before me. The picture has faded, but I think there were three parts to this path:

The Path of Love came first, then the Path of Light, then the Path of Life. It stretched for ever into the distance – did not Tolkien truly say, 'The road goes ever on and on,' it may take us eternity to travel, but yet perhaps it could take but an instant.

Finally I leave you with a short story of the ghost that is within all of us – the voice within.

EPILOGUE – A MOMENT IN TIME

I had gone alone up into the mountains – to be quiet, to think, not expecting to find anything. After all, God had deserted us, hadn't he? Every fresh discovery of science either removed the mysteries of existence, or worse still in these latter days, showed that nature had tinkered about through billions of years and eternities of space quite haphazardly, and we just pawns in the game.

As I sat there among the prominence and heights of the earth I realised I was being presumptuous and that I was little more than an ant. Did I have the wisdom to tell nature how to go about her business; could I do a better job? 'Rest a while,' said the silent voice, 'but then go back down, my little ant! You have seen, a faint glimpse perhaps; you have understood, a tiny grasp perhaps. For do you not feel this little blade of grass, this earth, this stone? Do you not feel? The time and space are but illusions, and only this precious moment of life exists.'

Life dwindled on. The daily grind at work, nights out in the pubs, the club on Saturday night – cards, darts, dominoes. Sunday rambles or games in the park; my father and one of my brothers died. I was depressed, and getting nowhere fast. Then came transforming moment of magic, a moment in time I would never forget. Loveliness radiated from her, sat round a bonfire barbecue on an autumn evening. She was as I dreamed she would be, she was as I knew she would be. Consciously, I only knew I must make her my own, somewhat reserved by nature I had no idea how! But the voice within her said, 'Yes, I am yours, do not worry; we have known each other before, and will do so again. Eternity is in this moment.'

> *Inside, my heart was singing:*
> *The moment we touch I will know you*
> *The thrill will shoot to my heart*
> *And all the long years of yearning*
> *Will be as naught.*

Once during our life together she said, "We know what love is. Even if we never had sexual intercourse again, the love we know would be sufficient to last us all our lives." Of course I, being the physical animal that I was, did not really cotton on to this idea, and prattled on about the importance of sex! I did not understand. Later on in years she suddenly said, "It will be worse for the one who is left." Again I did not understand. I could not think of anything worse than becoming ill and dying, being rather afraid of death myself. But when she was eventually taken from me, those words were to smite me with tremendous force.

I went back up the mountainside – and I spoke first. "I NOW FEEL," I shouted, half expecting God or an angel to answer. The little blade of grass half crushed beneath my foot stirred with life and held my gaze. 'Yes,' it said to me, "I know."

ADDENDUM 1

FRAGMENTS OF WISDOM

Sophia, or perhaps other advanced Great Ones, may sometimes help us in the night, when our brain is at rest and we are in subconscious mode. When we awake we probably have no recollection, or just a vague feeling or impression, for our conscious brain is busy again. If we awake during the night the recollection may be more vivid for a few moments, but being in a drowsy state we drop off to sleep again and all is forgotten. If however you have within reach pen and paper and put down the thoughts while they are still fresh in your mind, fragments of wisdom may be revealed to you. But also, in the night in our subconscious minds, we will often sense we are being tested, and may awake with a vague feeling that we have failed the test. Sometimes they may come simply to give us a subtle warning that we have gone astray, or a prompt to quicken the 'life within' – before it is too late.

We all have a guardian angel. Naive, unscientific? Well, the essence of science is to put things to the test. Therefore before you go to sleep tonight pray to your guardian angel and she will be with you, to watch over you, to guard and protect you – in accordance with what is ordained. Ask her to guide your way, to be with you always – and she will. If you believe then so shall it be. Do you not know this is so? Now that I have asked you that question I must ask you some more:

For whom does the bell toll?
Are you your brother's keeper?
Who is the stranger at the gate?
And do you now sense the sparrow's fall?

When you can answer these questions unhesitatingly and without any doubt in your heart then you will know who Sophia is, who I am, and who you are. Another way of viewing the guardian angel is to regard her as your conscience (your Jiminy Cricket). And yet another way is to realise that you have an inner self, a Master within. Remember there are many ways up the mountain side.

We are all living in a dream -
a dream of our own making.
You can learn to alter the dream.
Your dream is your conception of the world.

The lamb will still be here when
the lion has perished.
The blade of grass will crumble
the rocky mountain to dust.
Think then, where does the real strength lie?

Did I not create thee,
and put you in a book – the Book of Life.

ADDENDUM 2

I have written this little book from a male perspective, but I do not intend any sexism. One of the great advances of the twentieth century has been the establishment of the equality of men and women. A female reader may have to make slight alterations here and there. For instance she may view her guardian angel as a 'he', and any ghosts she encounters, sleeping or waking, she may conceive as predominately male! However, it matters little. In actual fact ghosts do not have bodies, they only seem to have them. No body, no brain; just what are they then? They are thoughts and desires floating in the 'aether.' Can they love each other? Not physically, not sexually. There is a great deal of difference between love and sex , which we gradually learn through life's experiences.

Eventually when all desire ceases are we anything at all? Occupying no time or space perhaps we are nothing. 'From dust we came and to dust we shall return' – it took humanity a long time to understand this truth. The stars are sprinkled like dust in the eternity of time and space, like sand on the seashore, and from those atoms everything, including us, came. And 'from nothing it came and to nothing it shall return,' one day we may come to understand that truth.

But that is a long way in the future perhaps and before then, in the present eternity of time and space, the Book unfolds, the dream continues. Are there some things, not physical, that will endure? Remember the Path, revealed by Soraya.

APPENDIX I

Although God is merely a concept of the human mind that does not necessarily mean that God does not exist. Our concepts of God are rather infantile, but a little step forward in maturity came with the gradual acceptance of One God. The concept will evolve as the human race evolves.

The 'big bang' is merely a connotation to attempt to describe the beginning of the universe. Science has been trying to understand it but finds it cannot do so; this is because science has little or no grasp of the immaterial. Infinity and eternity cannot exist in the material universe, but they do exist in the immaterial, from which this universe was breathed into existence. The immaterial is the nothing. It is also the all. Scientists may say this is just side-stepping the questions and the issues. But the immaterial can be experienced, even though it may be only for a moment. Mystics have sought this flash of enlightenment throughout the ages

The material universe contains many evidences of its immaterial birth, evident that is to the mystic. First you must remove the specks from your eyes, and open them. And where did this immaterial come from? This unconsciousness, this nothing, this Oneness and the All, this Power, this wondrous divine Being. It did not come from anywhere, for

I AM THAT I AM

Suggested further reading:
The poem 'Last Lines' by Emily Brontë.

APPENDIX 2

Man's place in the universe.

YEARS AGO
IN MILLIONS

14000	START-THEBIGBANG
12000	The First Stars born
4500	Earth was born
3000	Volcanoes. Methane/ammonia atmosphere
2500	Amino acid soup. BACTERIA
2000	Cellular life; amoeba
1000	Jellyfish and corals
750	Flatworms in the sea
600	Roundworms and molluscs
500	Squids, marine life. First land plants
400	First land animals – crabs, scorpions, millipedes INSECTS, Spiders, sharks and rays

YEARS AGO
IN MILLIONS

350	Flying insects. FISH. Oxygen risen to present level
300	Amphibians
250	DINOSAURS
200	BIRDS
150	Plants develop flowers
100	Shrews
65	Dinosaurs become extinct
25	GRASS
20	Grazing animals
10	Monkeys
4	Upright apes
2.5	PRIMITIVE MAN
0.2	HOMO SAPIENS (or saps like us!)

The timescale is vast and space is almost infinite – there are 125 billion galaxies and ten thousand billion billion suns.

APPENDIX 3:

THE ATOM

The atom consists of a nucleus of protons and neutrons, clustered tightly in a very small space, which constitutes the mass of the atom, and tiny circling electrons. It is actually about 99% space. The protons have a positive charge; the electrons are negatively charged. So that solid table that you see and feel is actually nearly all space!

What then gives the table and the physical world its apparent solidity? It is the electromagnetic.field produced between the nucleus and the circling electrons, and the interaction of your electromagnetic field and the objects overall electromagnetic field.

The electron has a charge of -1.6×10^{-19} coulombs. If this charge was much smaller the nucleus would hold the electrons less tightly and many atoms would then be unstable. If this charge was much greater the nucleus would hold the electrons more tightly, molecular compounds could not be formed, and so life would not be possible.

The electron is infinitesimally small, having a mass of 9.10×10^{-28} grams. The proton has a charge of $+1.60$

x 10^{-19} coulombs, and a mass of 1.67 x 10^{-27} kg. Neutrons are very similar to protons but without the electrostatic charge, and will decay into protons unless they are trapped inside an atomic nucleus.

The whole atom is extremely small. There are about one hundred thousand million million million molecules in a tablespoon of water. When atoms combine to form molecules it is the orbital waveforms that combine, the electrons themselves always repel one another.

BOOK 2

MYSTIC
GUARDIAN

'...one day perhaps you will come to love me.'

Sophia.

CONTENTS

FOREWORD

SCIENCE AND MYSTICISM

The particularised paths of science are now in this 21st century con verging ever so slowly towards the broader vista of the mystic path, although they use different terminologies. Scientists are attempting to discover how matter came into being from the energy released at the 'big bang'. The atom has been disintegrated into eight electronic particles and their corresponding anti-particles. Behind these particles lie tiny strings of vibrating energy. In reality nothing exists but vibrations, number, and their associated electro-magnetic fields. Science admits that a creative force has produced life, and given it a window of opportunity to know itself.

Science and mysticism are both after the same goals: To know what created the universe and how it operates, but science cannot admit any creator or God into the story, as it is not demonstrable and smacks of belief ratherthan fact. However there is a creative power in the universe whatever we wish to call it. Interpolating backwards in time the entire energy of the universe is condensed into a space smaller than a pinhead with an almost infinite density, which is an indescribable nonsense, unless perhaps it came from something immaterial, beyond the laws of physics. But science cannot as yet discourse on the immaterial either. According to quantum physics, Heisenberg's uncertainty principle, and Schrodinger's equations, anything and everything is possible but dependent on its probability. It is possible for example that there are an infinite number of parallel universes, but the probability is that there is only one. In any case only one need concern us!

Energy is quantised; so we find the electrons revolving around the nucleus can only have certain orbitals; also energy emission from a hot body occurs in quantum steps of hf, 2hf, 3hf, and so on, where h is Planck's constant. This ensures stability in the physical world we inhabit. However in the subatomic world, where particles are smaller than their quantum wavelengths, the particle behaves like a probability wave. This also means we never find a perfect vacuum, and the residual lambda vacuum energy provides a repulsive force to the attraction of the gravitational force. The cosmologists now think the self-reproducing inflationary universe has no beginning or end. It is worth noting that the theories and estimated numbers of science are forever changing, but the concepts of mysticism throughout history and many civilisations are remarkably similar and unchanging, as we shall see.

This little book presents a glimpse of the mystic vision of life. In this vision all is one, all mankind is one. Peace and Love are transcendent, and this can be achieved in just one moment of understanding, in the influx of nirvana. However, in man's present state of development it is more likely to take ten thousand years. This is because of mental immaturity, and because only a few travel the mystic path. In the mystic vision you and I are one. We may be very different physically, in our genetic make-up, in our clothes and worldly goods, in our talents if any! But deep within, in our real selves, we know we are one. And I love you, my brother. I love you, my sister, with all my heart.

This book is brief, for wisdom must come from within. No one can travel the mystic path for you. Do not ask anyone what any of the words mean. Ask only within your own heart, and gradually a still small voice from inside yourself will tell you. Some books are produced in a large heavy format with a thousand pages, and you lug the treasure home with you.

It has a long and great introduction or synopsis, and the book itself starts off in good style. Halfway through however and it feels as if the author is deliberately extending the story and it begins to be more woolly and abstruse. Three quarters through and you begin to flag, and it all ends in rather a damp squib. After all, there is no need for words when one grasps the truth.

PROLOGUE

THE TRAVELLER

In the first card of the Tarot – 0. The Fool – the seeker is represented as a young man or rambler striding off on the journey of life, full of hope, and carrying his rucksack or bag on his back. The sack is a burden but it is not too heavy to begin with. However as he travels on he starts to add things to his sack. The material things glitter, are new and enticing, especially those made of gold, and those that add to his standing as seen by others, to his fame and power. The burden grows heavier, but he takes little notice, saying to himself 'I am strong and healthy', and he greedily adds more lest others grab their share first.

And then he stumbles, the burden is weighing him down. But he cannot leave it now, others will steal it. Anyway, it has now stuck to him and will not let go. Looking into the mirror he is suddenly aware that the joyful carefree smile of hope and trust has gone, and that his happiest days were when he had possessed nothing. Yes, in those days now long gone he had trusted in something, hadn't he, something intangible. But just what was it?

PART ONE

The Path to Truth

First we will take a brief look at the path to truth from a mundane worldly viewpoint, and then approach it mystically from within.

RELIGION and POLITICS

Bias leads to the suppression of truth, and this is shown throughout the history of both religion and politics. Any organisation that is biased to one viewpoint only is going to be in error, for the truth becomes distorted. That which supports the preconceptions is retained and stressed and that which does not is manipulated, unexpressed or suppressed. As an example in religion one can cite the opposition of the Roman Catholic church to the scientific discoveries of Galileo and Darwin.

All religions are concepts of man. No one has ever spoken to God, for even God is merely a concept of man. How superstitions and religious rites became ingrained into the psyche of man has been well documented by Sir James George Frazer, in his work 'The Golden Bough.'

Because most political systems inwardly soon begin to sense they are not seeking any real truth they fear any opposing views and attempt to stifle the opposition by force. They tell themselves the ends justify the means, and this leads them to commit all manner of atrocities. The attempted extermination of the Jewish people by the

Nazis is just one of countless examples. Communism even tried to fetter science and music. To put fetters on the universal language of music is.like trying to chain the very soul of man. But the communists did not know that man had a soul, for they had lost their own. 'Fellow' human beings were just ants to be manipulated for the good of the colony.

Consider the body. Did we create it? Did we create any of the other animals, or any of the multitude of species that inhabit the earth? They were created over millions of years by Nature – the force of life. This force of life rules the universe. In man's puny attempts to understand it he called it God or the gods, and religions came into being. But they are narrow-minded, closed to real thought, and biased. If intolerance is added to this bias they become the very opposite to the force of life and evil is the result. The force of life is a much greater power, a much greater intelligence, and has a much greater nurturing love than our small minds.

Political systems have been devised by man to govern his way of life, but these too are straight-jacketed, closed to open thought, and biased. If intolerance is added to this bias evil is the result.

But the force·of life is completely open, a goodness, a kingdom of heaven spread out over the earth for all to see and be part of – but man does not see it!

Therefore we see that religion and politics are not paths to the truth for they are biased. In place of bias one should cultivate tolerance.

However, is it wise to become so tolerant that we countenance and appease evil? In the world's present state of evolution is it wise to let evil triumph? If that were so then we would have been subjected to the terrible regimes of Nazism or communism. Whether 'tis nobler in the mind to suffer the slings and arrows of outrageous fortune, or to take arms against a sea of troubles, and by opposing end them? Shakespeare, an astute observer of the human condition, posed this question. To appease evil is surely wrong. One must stand up, and be counted. We see that evil can exist in political regimes and in religions if they add intolerance to their already existing bias.

Although organised religion has been discredited here, it can still be very beneficial to meditate in the quietude and inward peace of the soul, for that is the real path to truth. This path will lead us to the Oneness, the oneness of everything, the oneness of you and me.

SCIENCE

The intelligent man pursues Truth through scientific investigation. untrammelled by religious or political narrow mindedness. The intelligent man has reached a stage of maturity where he takes responsibility for his actions. Science should be free to explore where it will. Governments, schools and universities should not restrict scientific endeavour into some perceived channels of economic gain or technological advance – it should be free to pursue knowledge for its own sake, for this is the way to Truth. Science is a gradual approach to the truth, so it is unlikely that it will ever know everything.

The human race must develop maturity and responsibility. This journey into the next phase of our evolution has already begun, the first step being the recognition of the responsibility to care for the planet we live on. Under communism the earth was being polluted at an ever-increasing rate, just to achieve economic advantage over others. Such political ideology is anti-truth, disguising evil as a necessity.

The observation by scientists that the ozone layer was being depleted by man's use of aerosols and refrigerants was the first jolt to make us think about the vulnerability of our planet both to what we do and to the vast forces of nature. However this is only a small beginning born out of necessity. We must learn to think not as a selfish individual, not as an egotistical nation or religion, but as an all-embracing mind, a universal mind that seeks no self-advantage, but seeks only truth. A mind that is free with no chains of religion or politics, but gives only life, light, and love to all. Expressing this another way, we should think and act in the same way that Nature does and be one with her.

THE CREATION – A BIT OF SCIENCE

Immediately after the big bang we have an extremely dense extremely hot ball of energy expanding outwards, containing closed loops or strings of energy vibrating at frequencies determined by the lengths of the strings. One could have a still simpler picture, as the mystics have always had, and say that in the beginning there were just positive and negative vibrations.

Where positive and negative vibrations superimposed on each other standing waves were produced giving rise to fundamental particles – electrons, positrons, neutrinos, and quarks. There are six kinds of quark – up, down, charm, strange, top, and bottom; and six antiquarks. A quark does not exist free by itself, but only in combination with other quarks.. Two up quarks and one down quark united to form protons, two down quarks and one up quark formed neutrons. The consequent union of electrons and protons produced hydrogen atoms, and the union of electrons, protons and neutrons gave rise to helium atoms.

The other elements were produced later on in the suns, which formed from the coalescing of the hydrogen and helium atoms under the force of gravity. The mass of particles depends on factors of energy distribution and momentum. Mass and energy are interchangeable according to the equation $e = mc^2$, where c is the speed of light. Exploding suns called supernovae distributed the elements and formed planets.

AND A LITTLE TRUTH

I, Nature am the creator, and I have nurtured you because you are my child. I love you as I love all my creation, and if you are one with me you will know the wonder of love, of light, and of life.

PHILOSOPHY

Philosophy is the love or pursuit of wisdom, first begun in Greece about 500 B.C. By a combination of reasoned argument and logical debate, contemplation and meditation, the ancient Greeks tried to arrive at an explanation of the world in which we live, to approach truth. Philosophy and science thrived in the Greek civilisation because they were not hidebound by religious fanaticism, looking on the gods on the mounts of Olympus and Parnassus as a powerful but reasonably friendly family of beings using mankind now and again as a toy to play with.

The first philosophers considered the question 'What is the underlying basis or foundation of the world.' The world was conceived as being composed of four elements – earth, air, water and fire. This is certainly true. Thales proposed that the primal element was water, and Anaximenes that it was air. In a marvellous insight however Anaximander thought that the basic element was boundless and infinite. Heraclitus came up with a concept far in advance of previous thinkers, asserting that all things were forever changing, in a state of flux. Plato later wrote that 'All is becoming, all things are in motion.' The Pythagoreans contended that number was the foundation of all things, and the only unchanging factor.

Democritus conceived the atom as the building block of matter, which centuries later was shown to be a remarkably accurate picture or representation. This was an age of great intellectual discoveries, using the mind alone, without any of the scientific apparatus and methods that we have today. How was this possible?

Socrates, in his philosophical arguments and debates, essayed to take all opinions into account, thus avoiding bias. Truths would eventually be brought out from within us. Virtue and wisdom could not be taught, but must grow from within, be found within oneself. Intuitive insights may come from within after the conscious mind, and then the subconscious mind, has dwelt upon a problem.

ONENESS

The path to Truth can be seen as a combination of scientific endeavour and the wisdom of the inner self. Everything has an inner self. When we see an object we see only its outer self. But it is actually composed of billions of atoms vibrating with energy. Electrons revolve around the nucleus in stepped energy levels, but we cannot say where an electron actually is at any point in time. The object, whatever it may be, stays true to its living inner self. In the life forms of plants and animals nature has allowed for variance and evolution, but they remain essentially true to their seed and their inner self, their raison d'etre.

Man has the mental power to choose, to vie with nature, to control his environment to some degree, to seek and explore. But if he is not true to his inner self he will not be at peace with himself. The inner self is not just the seed, not just the genes, for it is an intangible soul. If you are one with the soul then you have attained peace, heaven on earth.

The power and life of Nature is in every atom, every cell, everything. Nature reigns supreme. Man is just one of its creations, and he must live in accordance and harmony with Nature, and its many other creations. They and we are all one in Nature. The divine life and power of Nature tends to gradual evolution. But Nature herself has no set purpose, except to give life and nurture that life, for Nature is, Nature is already perfect. It gives life to all, and nurtures, protects, and evolves this life

Nature is the Word, giving life and nurture to all. Its rain falls on the just and the unjust, for it has perfect love, perfect giving. But any purposes are set by man. In his brief history he has set many purposes and laws, but they have been tainted through having false beliefs. He attempts to be just, but is hampered and deflected by the bias of politics and religion.

This bias leads to unjust treatment of our fellow men. What we do to another we do to ourselves. We used to enslave captured enemies, and cast people accused of any crimes into the vilest prisons, very likely to be tortured or rot to death. As short a time ago as 1750 AD those who through force of circumstances owed a little money or who stole a loaf of bread were imprisoned, often for life. By 1850 thousands of people were still being executed in one way or another for some crimes, often on circumstantial or biased evidence. In the 1940s there were the horrors of Nazi and Japanese prison camps. Our desire to punish and be cruel to others is hypocritical, based on fear, and unworthy of a mature human being.

In its present state of mental immaturity human society still needs protection against habitual criminals and religious fanatics, and these people should be isolated from society. Fraudsters and scammers should be given a taste of their own medicine by having to repay all of any stolen money and being heavily fined. Most other transgressors need to attend social rehabilitation centres to learn how to be right-thinking members of society, to be constructive not destructive. Also social responsibility should be taught in schools. These measures will do away with most imprisonment, and help to change the primitive human desire to inflict punishment on others, which originally arose in sacrificial rites to appease the gods.

Each of us has a path, a destination. Some of us have been through hell, maybe the hell of war, maybe the hell of mental depression. Some of us have been, perhaps still are, in the mire of filth, the filth of human vice; addicted or ensnared in the coils of over-indulgence in physical pleasure and desires. But out of the soil green shoots of life may yet evolve. By living in hell, and struggling out of the filth and mire, we slowly attain a little understanding, and a little bit of moral strength to regain the path and travel a little further thereon. Stay true to this moral strength and inner conscience, despite all the derision of the world. Stay true. For that is where the real strength lies, that is where the Truth is.

In a general sense mankind's mission is to actualise the ideals he somehow knows exist within, deep within himself, within the infinite UN-CONSCIOUS. The infmite unconscious is the soul that science knows nothing about, and has no understanding of. In our individual lives our long term mission is to fmd and travel the path that leads to Oneness with the soul. When we are at one with Nature and with the soul within then we will be at peace and can cease our searching. For most people the immediate mission is to pursue one's interests, to develop any talent we may have been given, perhaps to raise a family, to help others in friendship and love, to live our life to the best of our ability. And to learn the lessons of life appropriate to our present stage of development.

It is wise not to squander it – for it is loaned to us for just a short spell, and it depends on just one breath.

The moon, the stars – they belong to anybody.
The sunshine, the wind, the rain –
    they too belong to anybody.
Light, life, love – how rich this anybody is,
    if he only realised it.

STEPS ON THE PATH

STEP I

It is morning, the dawn of a new day. Open your eyes, what do you see? There is the planet Earth in all its glory, part of a vast universe, and you are a part of it. It came from nothing, yet it contains almost infinite energy. This energy first mani festing in the universe as positive and negative electrons, evolved to form protons and atoms of hydrogen, the suns and the planets. In our sun alone there are 10 to the power of 57 atomic particles; in the universe there are at least 10 to the power of 22 suns and even more planets. The suns indeed are the 'lamps of God,' radiating light into the darkness, and also nurturing life.

We think of ourselves as quite clever and 'top dog' of our patch, and sometimes even imagine ourselves to be rulers of the universe. Although we can manipulate matter not one of us could ever create one single atom. This Earth teems with life, that has evolved over the millennia from what we look upon as non-life. Although we can procreate life, and even manipulate life-forms, not one ofus could ever create a single spark of life. Let us consider the life-force within us. Did we create it?

It has been given to us, bestowed on us, but we did not create it, and have little power over it. The conclusion to be drawn is that we are privileged to share in this creation, this Life. We are part of it, and to discover our part in it we set forth on this Path.

Because there were many things early man could not explain he devised the idea of gods having ascendancy over the affairs of men, and various religions came into being. One sees the emergence of those wishing to dominate by religious power.

Religions gradually evolved the conept of one God. However by its very birth from ignorance religion does not, even though it might profess it, possess absolute truth. The denial of the scientific truth of Herschel, Galileo and Darwin shows quite the opposite. The path we are on is the search for truth, and we will not find it in any one religion. However, religion may help us along the way for a space. There are some good thoughts in all religions, mainly originating from the great personages after whom most of these religions are named, but no one theology knows the whole truth. To think so leads you to become biased and intolerant. Biased people lose their grasp on rational thinking, and they are led further and further off the path.

What we need to get started is the initial desire to strive upwards, to better ourselves, and to help others. We must step onto the Path.

STEP 2

Some paths come to an impasse or a dead-end, and many other paths gradually merge into clearer broader paths. The Path we seek is even higher up – it is the Path of Truth. To step on this Path we need to do away with beliefs, because beliefs cannot be substantiated. Men have believed many things, but eventually they are all shown to be false.

Then we need to investigate all the phenomena of nature in a scientific manner. It is only by the discoveries of science that we progress in our knowledge of the universe. It is by progressing in our knowledge of the universe that we can approach the Truth and take our right part in Creation, and in the Story of Life.

STEP 3

Whilst we may pursue scientific investigation we must not lose sight of the greater whole in the complex of particulars. Science is only part of the story. The next step is to open our eyes and actually see the greater whole. Most of us have eyes but we do not see. There are many specks in our eyes that obscure the vision. Many of these specks are faults we see and criticise in others, but do not realise that we have these very self-same faults in ourselves. The vision is also smeared and blurred by faulty understanding, caused by egotistical traits in the personality. If we remove the specks, and forget the self, what will we see? What will we see?

The mystic path is the journey, the road, the way that leads one to enlightenment, when your eyes are opened and at last you see.

STEP 4

Step 4 is the realisation of the importance of love, the

opening of love in your heart, and its magical power to transcend and transform all else.

Let the light of love radiate from your being so that it illuminates all that is before it, and reveals it in a new light and gives you a new understanding.

STEP 5

With Love and Understanding you will now have Life. But of course you had life all the time – it had been freely given to you. But you did not realise it in the right way then, you did not know what it was, what a magnificent gift it was. You did not know that heaven is here and now, and not somewhere up above in some future time.

In the Oneness and the ALL
There is only this moment.
There is no past and future
Nor time and space.
Only the now exists.

PART TWO

Aspiration Towards Nobility of Mind

CHAPTER 1

WHAT IS A MYSTIC?

Mysticism is concerned with visionary experience and prophesy, and can be defined as the spiritual quest for union with the divine. A mystic is a seeker, a seeker after the meaning of life, the meaning of existence. What lies behind the appearance of things? He seeks to tap into the energies that run the universe, to delve into the soul of man, to know oneself. In high-flown terms he is an ontologist who delves into the science of being or reality. He is also a student of cosmogony, seeking to know who or what created the universe. However, you do not have to be intellectually clever to be a mystic. It is not something you choose to be or to do, rather it chooses you when you are ready. We may take Jacob Boheme (1575–1624) as an example.

Born in Germany to poor parents Jacob Boheme (or Bohme) looked after sheep as a boy, and later on became a humble cobbler. However, after having a religious experience at the age of twenty five he devoted much of his time to.meditation on divine things. In 1612 he published his 'Aurora', a book of revelations and meditations on God, man, and nature.

The work was condemned by the ecclesiastical authorities, and he was cruelly persecuted. He held that God must be experienced directly in mystical illumination, and he then later developed a complete theosophical system. Theosophy is said to be characterised by esoteric doctrine and an interest in occult phenomena. He also wrote other works that had a great influence on later intellectual movements, such as Idealism and Romanticism. Another noted mystic was Meister Eckhart, a Dominican who wrote on the relationship between God and humanity. He was charged with heresy in the year 1320.

A mystic is a person who has been prepared, who is now ready to hear the call of the inner voice, and his feet are set on a path. This path is a journey of the mind and soul to find illumination, the meaning and purpose of life, to find unity with the divine. In allegorical tales the mythical King Arthur and certain of his knights travelled the path, seeking the Holy Grail, and to attain equanimity. We too will take this mystic path. First we must follow the urges of the soul and subconscious_ mind, be called by an inner voice, and set our feet on the path.

CHAPTER 2

MYTHS AND LEGENDS

We are roughly halfway through the life of this planet, and we can make a guesstimate that we are halfway through our evolution too.

It has taken nature almost 2000 million years to evolve us, so we may still have a long way to go. We have risen from primitive apelike creatures. even from the dawn of life, for we see evidence of this in the gills of the human embryo.

We endeavour to strive upwards to future goals. Greater powers than us created this vast universe. Certainly great forces and energies exist locked up in every atom. This has given rise to many myths and legends of creation and the gods. They and their symbols have become embedded in the psyche of man – in the collective unconscious.

They show our yearning to raise ourselves up in moral strength and wisdom. The soul has a desire for light, and an irrepressible urge to rise out of primal darkness. Of course, there were also many super stitious beliefs which science has since shed light on and banished.

THE SYMBOLIC JOURNEY

According to the renowned psychologist C. G. Jung

161

mankind has a Collective Unconscious, which is deep down in all of us. Inborn intuitive archetypes are contained in our collective unconscious and memory, and are closely related to our instincts. These universal archetypes reveal themselves in mythological images and symbols. as for instance the wise spirit or wise old man, which is portrayed as Merlin in the Arthurian legends and as Gandalf in *The Lord of the Rings*. They also often have sacred emotions or feelings attached to them. If we bring them into our consciousness we can journey through man's most significant leaps in his psyche's evolution which have been encoded there in evocative symbols.

In the mythologies of many countries and cultures we see the development of the hero figure, who can fraternise with the gods due to his valour. Celtic tribes settled in Britain from 700 BC onwards. When the Romans arrived the Celts were driven westwards. The name Britain derives from the Cymric language of old Wales, in which the whole Celtic island was called B'rith-ain. In Celtic lore the Otherworld is the source of wisdom, the place of their gods. Whoever journeys to this Otherworld becomes more than mortal. They pictured it as a place where great deeds could be accomplished, and the hero's life perfected. In the Otherworld lies the fountain or well of wisdom. The queen of the Otherworld invites us to drink of the fountain so our inner faculties will awaken and become clear, and she gives us three gifts. Our real inner name; a talisman, or a tool or an implement to help us on the path; and bids us look into the waters of the fountain where they run into a quiet pool, and where we will clearly see ourselves performing some part of our true future destiny. Tolkien made use of this myth in *The Lord of the Rings*, when Frodo meets Galadriel in Lothlorien she asks him to look into the basin of water, that is the mirror of Galadriel; the whole of this book is full of such mythological allusions, which is the secret of its success.

Poets were also deemed to have access to the Otherworld, and they carried a branch with tinkling bells, which was a symbol of the everliving tree, that grew in the Blessed Isles of the Otherworld. The Birds of Rhiannon sat on this tree, and whoever heard the song of these birds fell into a timeless state.

The Irish Celts named their land EIRE, after the goddess Eriu. To the ancients the land and the gods were one. The four elements – air, fire, earth and water – were the most powerful manifestations of the gods. The Great Mother was nature or the earth. The king was also wedded to the land; it was very important to find the true king in order to have a prosperous land. Celtic mythology recognised the interdependence of the whole of nature, and that there was no beginning or end to life and creation. God was both male and female, the Father – Mother in the heavens.

After the Romans left Britain, the Celtic priesthood ordained Arthur as High King of the Britons, and he ruled throughout the latter half of the sixth century. He was descended from Ygerne, high queen of of the Celtic kingdoms, and Morgaine was his half-sister. Morgaine was the personification of the Lady of the Lake, who ruled in Avalon in the Otherworld, with her nine 'sisters'. She may have been derived from the water nymphs of Breton folklore. Later in the Arthurian legends she is somewhat denigrated as Morgan le Fay, because she sides with Mordred against Arthur, and where she is regarded as a sorceress.

Arthur's grandmother was Viviane I, whose husband was Taliesin the Bard, the druidic Merlin in the first half of the sixth century. Taliesin died in 540 AD, and the title of Merlin went to Emrhys of Powys, who was to feature later in Arthurian legends. The Guardians of the Celtic Isle were called Pendragons, and the dragon emblem subsequently be the Red Dragon of Wales.

The legendary Arthur, who expressed chivalry and nobility, first appeared in 1147, in the work *Historia Regum Brittanniae* by Geoffrey of Monmouth. In 1175 in five related tales Chretien de Troyes wrote of Guinevere, Lancelot, and Camelot. Cistercian monks produced another five tales of Arthur during the period 1215 to 1235; these featured Galahad, the son of Lancelot, and Elaine. The Welsh *Red Book Of Hergest* also featured Arthur and the many Welsh knights, kings and princes, during the times when he held his court at Caerleon on the river Usk. The stories of King Arthur and the Knights of the Round Table that now inspire the English and Welsh peoples have become absorbed into the collective unconscious and are now part of their psyche. His mother was Igraine, wife of the Duke of Tintagel, and his father King Uther Pendragon. Excalibur, the sword which was given to Arthur by the Lady of the Lake, is a symbol of the hero, of heroic deeds, and of kingly power.

Avalon was the sacred island in the Otherworld,

where the sword Excalibur was forged, and to which Arthur was taken after being mortally wounded in the battle with Mordred. He establishes the noble reign of the Knights of the Round Table, and is aided by the wise old man, personified by Merlin. And for a short space his reign brings peace and stability to the land and its people.

Each year at the feast of Pentecost the knights assembled to renew the vows of allegiance, instituted by Arthur. They pledged not to be cruel or to commit murder, but to be merciful to those who asked for mercy, or they would face banishment from the Round Table. Also not to take on battles for a wrongful cause or for worldly goods, and to come to the aid of all ladies, damsels, and gentlewomen. In total there were 140 knights of the Round Table, but it is very unlikely to have been big enough to accommodate them all. Most of the knights would be away on quests and other adventures, and taking part in tournaments. There was one empty seat at the table, called the Siege Perilous, which was kept reserved for one totally pure in heart. No one had ever had the audacity to sit in this seat.

Various knights are personifications of archetypes in the unconscious, and we may look at a few of their characters here.

There is BEDIVERE, the loyal and faithful one, who was the companion of Arthur, and we will say more of him later.

PERCIVAL, guileless but good, who makes mistakes and almost succumbs to temptation. He appears to derive from the Welsh hero Peredur, who died in 580 AD. By living the noble and knightly life and persevering on the path, he eventually gains spiritual development. He goes on the quest for the Holy Grail with Galahad and Sir Bors, and eventually they reach the castle of the Fisher King. Here we must understand that the Holy Grail, or Sangreal, is not a material thing, but it is a spiritual condition, a mystical state that has to be *achieved*. The fisher-king in this instance is Joseph of Arimathea, eldest brother of Jesus, also known as James.

LANCELOT is cured of his madness by the grail, and Lancelot's brother Sir Ector, and Sir Percival are healed of their wounds; but Percival is told he is not yet ready to receive the Sangreal. According to Malory, the holy vessel Sangreal is a symbol of the blood of Jesus Christ, which was brought into this land by Joseph of Arimathea. He also says that Lancelot, whose mother was Viviane II, was eighth in succession from Jesus Christ, and GALAHAD ninth. Lancelot surpassed in manhood and prowess all others, but in spiritual matters he had many his better, for he had too much pride in and reliance on his physical attributes, that nature had given him. Apart from this, Lancelot was the flower or epitome of knighthood; valiant, gallant, courteous, merciful; without lustful desire of the flesh, throughout his life having no eyes for a woman save Guinevere.

King PELLAM of Listeneise fought with the knight Balin inside the latter's castle. The castle roof and walls fell on them, and they were trapped for three days. Pellam suffered from his injuries for many years, until he was.healed by Galahad. Pellam was descended from Joseph of Arimathea, who settled in Britain around 60

AD. Joseph had four children, and is said to be buried at the abbey in Glastonbury. Arthur's grandmother Viviane I was also descended from Joseph. A vision of Joseph and his angels administering the mass came to Galahad just before he died.

Sir PELLEAS, a noble and valiant knight, fell in love with the Lady Ettard, who scorned him and treated him despicably for a long time. He was on the point of killing himself, or dying of grief from a broken heart for this unrequited love, when he was rescued by NIMUE, one of the Damsels of the Lake. It is the Holy Spirit that heals the broken hearted (see Isaiah 61: 1). Malory says he wed Nimue, though in truth the Lady of the Lake and her nine 'sisters' or damsels are more beings of the Spirit – who inhabit the Isle of Avalon in the Otherworld – than mortals. In like manner Sir Gareth wed the Dame Lionesse, who was said to possess magic rings, and Sir Gaheris wed the damsel Linet, who had healing powers. Pelleas was made a Knight of the Round Table by Arthur, and later joined the quest for the Sangreal. Sir BORS de Ganis, nephew of Lancelot, was a pure knight who had spiritual visions whilst in the castle of King Pelles, who was a cousin of Joseph. He too joined Galahad on the quest.

GALAHAD, the son of Lancelot, is the personification of purity. After Galahad had been installed in the Siege Perilous at the high feast of Pentecost, the light of the Holy Ghost shone in onto the Knights of the Round Table, and every knight saw each other with a new vision, for every man seemed fairer than heretofore, and they were all struck dumb. All the knights then pledged to set out on the quest for the Holy Grail, and are tempted by pride of the ego, and by pleasures of the flesh, and one by one their vision faded and they failed the quest. Bors and Percival are also tried by temptations, but they finally win through, and together with Pelleas and Galahad, achieve the Sangreal. Galahad however, had then no more wish to remain in this mortal life, but chose to end it and live in the spiritual realm.

Arthur is then beset by troubles. There is the dissension and division from his kin Mordred, and the infidelity of his wife Guinevere. He remains, however, noble and chivalrous, for he has learnt the secret of equanimity, that forgives all. After that he had been mortally wounded, on Arthur's command Excalibur was thrown back into the lake by Sir Bedivere, albeit after he had twice been tempted to keep it. There came an arm and a hand above the water, and caught the sword, brandished it three times, and then vanished. This enduring and captivating scene is immortalised in the beautiful and eloquent imagery of Alfred Lord Tennyson in his poems. Bedivere then carries Arthur onto a barge wherein sits Morgan le Fay with the nine damsels of the lake, including Nimue, for to sail to Avalon to tend his wounds, and Bedivere was left lamenting at the waterside. However, as Arthur could not be healed physically in this world, a short while later Bedivere finds Arthur's newly dug grave at Glastonbury.

Yes, Arthur, you inspire us with your valour, your nobility, your chivalry. We feel one with you, and know that you are our rightful King. You fight with us against the invaders, and all our enemies. The strains of Jerusalem echo here, that stir the heart with memories and hope. But just who are our real enemies, Arthur? They too are within, and go under the names of pride, egotism and selfhood.

Wherein lay the power of the tales of Arthur and his knights to enthral? Then one night the truth came to me. Mary Magdalene, who may have been the wife of Jesus, bearer of the true knowledge, was the real Lady of the Lake. She had escaped from Roman persecution and settled in Gaul, in Aquitaine, and area west of Toulouse. Lancelot du Lac was her descendant, and Arthur was descended from Joseph of Arimathea, elder brother of Jesus. They truly are a part of the mystic path.

A KNIGHT'S JOURNEY

And on a day in the green pastures and meadows rode Sir Arathain seeking repose, for although still young he had been through many adventures just previous to this time. Coming to a copse where goodly fruits grew, he dismounted and sat down to rest. He partook a little of the fruit and immediately felt a little sleepy. Anon a damsel stood before him.

'Greetings, Sir Knight, what do you so far from your home?'

'I have had some arduous adventures of late, and sought rest, that is all I seek, fair one.'

'A small request indeed, but this can be a dangerous land for a lone wanderer. Angels you may find, but there are also sorceresses and powerful giants.'

'I have not yet been found wanting in battle,' replied

Arathain. 'If you need my succour, and set me a task I will perform it faithfully.'

'I thank you for your fair words, but I myself have no need for your valour.' And with that she vanished. A strange land indeed, mused Arathain, as he fell asleep.

He awoke refreshed, and the sun still shone in an azure sky, and so he mounted his steed and rode on in high hopes. He came to another copse of trees and was riding through when he heard a voice calling to him from up above.

'Help me Sir Knight, if thou wilt for I cannot get down.'

He straightway clambered up the tree, and helped the maiden down. 'Come with me, bold Sir Knight.'

The maiden was comely indeed, beautiful, and her smile enticing, as she led him into the woods.

'I offer you my service, but more than that I cannot give, for I have given my heart to the fair Megaine.'

'And where might this lady be?'

'In my own country, a long way from here alas.'

'Then she will never know what happens here, my love,' and she kissed him. In that sensuous kiss he was lost, his body ached for love, for culmination of desire. They disrobed, and lay on the sward together, for once the desire was set in motion there was no turning back. And a long time later, although the world had seemed to stand still, he returned to his senses, and the maiden had gone.

Feelings of remorse and shame began to obtrude on

his mind. He had betrayed his precious love Megaine. Would she ever forgive him?

He was dejected and felt tired and weak. And it was then that the giant Brazon appeared, and he was a strong man, and he challenged Arathain. 'I trust you will allow me to dress and arm myself,' said the knight. 'Attire yourself anywise you wish, it will make no difference to me, for I am invincible.'

Arathain jumped up and put on his armour, and horsed himself, but the giant was on foot. Then the battle commenced. First they fought with spears, and Arathain had the better. But the giant also wielded a cudgel in his left hand, and Arathain was unhorsed by a savage buffet on the side of his helmet from the cudgel. Then Arathain drew his sword and fought long and hard: but because the giant was strong, and Arathain had been weakened by the sorceress maiden, who had taken away his self-respect and chastity, he was at the last defeated by the giant, and taken to the giant's castle and thrown into the dungeons. The giant hung Arathain's shield on a tree before the castle gates, amongst many other such, of knights he had defeated. This was Arathain's first taste of defeat; its bitterness was hard to take, and he knew its cause. He had lost the valour of purity, and was filled with remorse. If he could only regain his strength he would fight that giant again, for it would be better to die fighting than to endure this shame.

'Why did I ever stray into this land, before I was ready to face such ordeals,' he bemoaned. And he prayed for God to forgive him.

Then one day a damsel came bearing food.

'The angels have heard your prayer. Eat of this and regain your strength. One other thing I can tell you is that your sword lies in the second chamber on the floor above.'

He was overjoyed by the visit of this strange damsel, but how to get out of the prison remained a seemingly unsurmountable problem. He rattled on the bars of the cell as hard as he could. Eventually Brazon came down the steps roaring.

'Be quiet, or I will silence you. What is amiss?'

'You defeated me by unfair means, when I was in a weak state, and not prepared for you,' he taunted. 'Challenge me again if you dare.'

'Why should I, when you are already my prisoner?'

'Because I do not believe you are as powerful and invincible as you boast that you are.'

'I warn you,' thundered the giant, 'I am stronger than ever if l am riled, puny mortal, and will slay you without mercy.'

'Prove it then.'

At this the giant removed the bars from the cell, and made to grab Arathain, who eluded his grasp, and ran up the steps to where his sword was hung. The giant followed, arming himself with cudgel, and ball and chain.. For all the giant's strength he was slow and cumbersome, and Arathain was able to dodge his blows, and continue to prick him sorely with the sword. Eventually Brazon weakened from loss of blood from his many cuts, and fell to the floor begging for mercy. Arathain bound him with cords, and departed hence. That damsel was right, and spoke truly, he mused, one needs guidance in this enchanted place, or one may fall into unsuspected traps. I saw the vanity in him, but did not see it in myself.

And he came to a riverside where sat some water nymphs, and they were naked and defenceless.

'Are you not afraid to be so, in this strange land?' he asked.

'This is our home, but you should not really be here. Although you have conquered the giant you are out of your depths. You should be back in your homeland, trying to be worthy of your true love, and to cherish and protect her. For your homeland is filled with much more evil than is present here. The only evil here is that which you bring with you.'

'But how do I get back there?'

'Follow the river downstream, till you come to the ships in the bay, and a boat may take you back to the mainland. But beware, there may be perils on the way.'

He journeyed on, but then a tributary into the river appeared in the way, and the path diverted away to the left side. Following this he found himself in a dark wood. And the wood nymphs whispered, 'What are you doing in this country, stranger?'

'Just passing through,' he answered.

'But where is your light, and your protection?'

'How do you mean?'

'To live in this country you must bring an inner light, and you must be armed with Truth.'

'Perhaps you can show me the way out then.'

'We cannot help you, for we stay in our woods.'

So he travelled on; becoming more and more entangled and lost in the darkness. Ghostly shapes assailed him. 'He has a suit of armour on, but he has no protection,' came the whispers on every side, and he began to grow afraid. Then a light came towards him, and when it drew near he saw it was one of the damsels of the island.

'If you had been able to ascend higher in the spirit you would have been able to soar over these obstacles; but come, I will lead you to safer ground.'

'Yes, I was in great need of you,' he replied.

She led him through the trees to where a narrow wooden bridge crossed the stream, and he thanked the damsel.

It is perilous to enter before our time, before we are ready.

CHAPTER 3

THE QUEST

Alchemy is the search for healing self-knowledge, the pursuit of spiritual wisdom, and the magical procedures for the rebirth of the soul. It is the doctrine of human perfectibility through enlightenment, symbolised by the quest for the philosophers stone, and the search for the Holy Grail. This doctrine was deemed heretical by the Roman Church, yet it is far older and more profound than anything this Church has to offer. The Holy Grail is derived from Sang Real – the Blood Royal; and at one level to seek for the Sangreal is to seek for the lineage of Jesus; on another level of understanding to seek for the Holy Grail is to seek for the Christ Spirit, the Holy Ghost, the Holy Word of God. The philosophers stone is a term for the inner soul of man and its enlightenment. This quest, which is the mystic path, was hidden in alchemical symbols because of the persecution of all 'non-orthodoxy' by church and state, especially by the Roman Catholic Church during the period of Inquisition.

The Inquisition first appeared in 1231 under Pope Gregory IX. The use of torture was approved by Pope

Innocent IV in 1252. The Spanish Inquisition was authorised by Pope Sixtus IV in 1478, and the first Grand Inquisitor was Thomas de Torquemada during the period 1487 to 1498. Almost two thousand people were burned at the stake during his tenure. Inquisitions were carried out in many countries over a very long period, particularly in the guise of witchfinder-generals. Thousands of innocent people were put to death. The Inquisition did not entirely disappear until around 1800.

When intolerance is added to bias evil is the result, and here we will examine one instance of this, although there have been many such in human history. This instance was so terrible that a word came into the dictionary to describe it. Over the centuries since these events have been hushed up, and the word not now often used, but it should be proclaimed in the same way as nazism is, as a blot upon the human race that it will have to atone for. That word is catharsis.

The Cathars lived in the Languedoc area, south of Montpelier in what is now southern France. The mediaeval walled town of Carcassonne was their main stronghold. Just to the east is Saintes-Maries de la Mer in the Camargue, where it is believed Mary Magdalene, Mary Salome, and Mary Jacobe landed with Joseph of Arimathea about 44AD. Mary Magdalene died in 63AD at Aix-en-Provence, leaving her mystical knowledge to the Cathar community. Today Saintes-Maries de la Mer is a pilgrimage destination for gypsy communities who gather annually for a religious festival in honour of Saint Sarah who was possibly a servant of the three Marys.

Afraid of this knowledge, the Roman Catholic

church, under Pope Innocent III in 1209 declared the Cathars to be heretics, and over the next 35 years thousands were put to death, culminating in the massacre at the seminary of Montsegur in 1244, where more than 200 Cathars were put up on stakes and burned alive. This wholesale slaughter of an innocent community of kind and right-living people who never harmed another human being beggars belief.

In establishing the religion of Christianity the Roman Catholic church had appropriated the teachings of Jesus to their own designs. At council meetings it had declared certain biased concepts that could not now be changed, such as the position of Peter as head of the Church, the male dominance factor in society, and the inferior position of woman. Thus it was opposed to any veneration of Mary Magdalene, and wanted to demote her to a minimal role in the Christian story.

A little later on Philippe IV of France and his puppet Pope Clement V began the persecution of the Knights Templar. The Order was outlawed in 1312, and its grand master burned at the stake in 1314. This was because the Knights Templar had become rich and powerful, and Philippe is said to have been in their debt. Further, the Knights had tried to retrieve the Ark of the Covenant from Jerusalem during their crusades and the Church was afraid their own fabrications would be exposed. Again, on the 24th August 1572, three thousand protestants were slaughtered in Paris, and another twelve thousand elsewhere in France.

The ecclesiastical authorities, when founding the Church of Rome, held the view that God was male, and that women were somehow inferior. From this one error came bias and intolerance, whereas it was clearly obvious even to primitive man that God and nature were both male and female.

However intolerance did not just belong to the Roman Church. The protestant Puritans under Oliver Cromwell were also extremely intolerant and committed similar atrocities. It is a human trait of the ego, which is full of fears and seeks to protect itself.. Also, one has to put these actions into the context of the age, and it is part of the religio-politico power wrangling that still goes on even in modern times. It is all part of the outer world, the domain of Caesar and of Satan. When you switch from the ego to the inner mystic path, as exemplified by Jesus and the Essenes, Mary Magdalene and the Cathars, the Knights Templar, and the Buddhists, then intolerance and bias are supplanted by love, right-thinking, and integrity. It is surely ironic that religions often do the very opposite of what the avatars themselves came into the world to teach.

To C. G. Jung the philosopher's stone was a transmuting agent to accomplish the unity of opposites, a spiritual transformation, and it also symbolised the fully individuated self, which is produced after old structures have been transformed, the male and female parts of ourselves resolved, body and soul united. The philosophers stone was the whole developed united Self, and Christ was the collective image of this Self.

The pursuit of the philosophers stone is akin to the quest for the Holy Grail in Arthurian legends. It is to seek for the divinity that resides deep within us. Indeed it resides within all things. This searching into the soul of man is also shown in *The Secret of the Golden Flower* (1668) written by the Chinese Taoist Lu Yan. In this work the flower represents opening into light, the awakening of the inner self. It uses a meditation technique known as 'turning the light around', the switching from the limited realm of the conscious mind and its conditioning to dwelling in the 'original mind', and letting the light shine from within. By regulated breathing and calmness of mind one enters into uninterrupted quiet, then emptiness, then freedom from desire.

THE TAROT

The many inequalities in human life lead to traits of character – all of which play their parts. All are deserving of love. We are all on that elusive quest for the secret of life, which has been symbolised in the deck of cards known as the Tarot. The Tarot cards symbolise various stages on the mystic path.

0. The Fool
This card represents the seeker or traveller. He is the young man striding off on the journey of life, full of hope, but carrying a burden on his back. The burden may diminish as he travels and learns the lessons of life, or it may grow if he fills it with egoistic greed and the material things of this world.

1. The Cobbler or Magician
Represents self awareness and acquired skills. He has an array of tools set out on his table, and is the master of crafts.

2. The High Priestess
Represents inner perception. The book in her lap represents esoteric wisdom and divine law. Associated

with the goddess Juno, who was both queen of heaven, and queen of the dead. In Celtic lore and Arthurian legend, the queen of Avalon.

3. The Empress
Stands for abundance, wealth, renewal and rebirth. She holds the sceptre, the symbol of power, but it is surmounted by a cross to signify that spiritual power rules over temporal might. She is also linked to the fruitfulness of Mother Earth.

4. The Emperor
Represents leadership, authority, and government. Also force and dominance, his helmet linking him to Mars, the god of war.

5. The Hierophant
He is shown as a religious father, blessing and inspiring his flock. He has an innate goodness. The triple cross he carries is said to be a symbol of the papacy, whereas the Maltese cross on his glove is a symbol of the Knights Hospitalers, who cared for the sick during the Crusades. The card also indicates a sincere applied vocation.

6. The Lovers
This card represents choice or dilemma, such as between idealistic love and physical attraction, between love and career, or between vice and virtue. It depicts a young man who must choose between the two women on either side of him.

7. The Chariot

Represents victory and achievement after effort and struggles. Winning through after trials by fire, air, earth, and water – represented by the four pillars. The charioteer's epaulettes represent the opposing forces of the carnal and spiritual. The two horses represent the emotions and physical passions which need to be controlled.

8. Justice

Represents fairness and honesty. The scales represent balanced judgement and upholding of the law. All the symbols are in pairs, symbolising the weighing of good and evil, except for the sword which is double-edged, one edge to condemn and the other to save.

9. The Hermit

The wise old man, Merlin of the Arthurian legends. He resides in our subconscious, to proffer us advice, to show us glimpses of the future, to guide us on the path. His staff represents the strength of the divine on which he can rely. He is also said to depict Old Father Time. His lantern is a symbol of the inner light or wisdom that guides the traveller on the right path, in the search for wisdom and truth. The hermit also denotes a person who is at that stage on the path of being an observer of the world and of life, without wishing to participate in it.

10. The Wheel of Fortune

The symbol of destiny, and rising and declining fortunes. The figures are tied to the wheel, sometimes ascending and evolving, sometimes falling back down. It also symbolises the Buddhist eternal round of reincarnation from which they cannot escape.

11. Strength
Stands for the triumph of the positive forces over the negative, of love over hate, of the spiritual over the material. It also represents the strength of the human spirit. She is plainly dressed to symbolise that purity is her underlying strength.

12. The Hanged Man
The hanged man willingly sacrifices himself with serenity, in order to achieve regeneration. The two pruned trees or saplings imply renewed growth to come.

13. Death
The implacability of fate and death for us all. However, it can also denote a fresh start or a new awareness. And it symbolises the end of an old life, and the rebirth or awakening of one's soul.

14. Temperance
This card denotes moderation and the middle way. The winged figure is an angel wearing a rose, the symbol of perfection. She is blending the liquids in two jugs, symbolising the harmonising of the spiritual and the material. This uniting of heaven and earth is also shown by the air above, and the land and plants below.

15. The Devil
This card implies destruction, and self-indulgence. It

also, of course, means evil, and human bondage to evil, for the Devil has dominion in this world. Of the horned and helmeted imps, one is female and the other male, suggestive of excessive carnal passion. The card gives a hint of possible redemption – if one strives to overcome evil. The Devil or Satan has a definite role to play in the scheme of things, given to him by God.

16. The Tower
Although showing a strong tower, it is struck by a lightning bolt, and its inhabitants sent hurtling to the ground. The card thus denotes sudden upheaval and change. It symbolises the pride and ambition of the ego overthrown, so that enlightenment may afterwards enter; or that one may begin again with a new perspective on life.

17. The Star
The themes of this card are hope, optimism and love, represented by the nude young girl, the birds and trees. The large star is thought to represent cosmic energy. Again, the waters from two pitchers are blended, one containing the water of life nourishing the material parts, and the other containing the spiritual water of the soul. The card thus signifies the unification of the two realms or planes, and rebirth.

18. The Moon
This card implies fluctuation. It can also impart intuition, imagination, and creativity.

19. The Sun

The sun sheds its power and warmth on all, and this card implies success and happiness.

20. Judgement

Implies resolution and reward. It also symbolises the cycle of birth and death. The trumpet of Saint Michael summons the dead souls to be weighed at the final judgement. The three figures shown emerging from the grave are naked, implying that they can conceal nothing.

21. The World

This final card is a joyous celebration of success, of completion,the culmination of all our seekings and strivings; and the achievement of wholeness, after the initiate into the mysteries, the traveller on the mystic path, has successfully passed through all the ordeals.

Please note that the use of tarot cards as a means of forecasting a person's future is not a practice advocated by mystics.

PART THREE

LIFE
Fleeting Yet Eternal

CHAPTER 4

THE NATURE-NURTURE DEBATE

Living organisms are essentially genetic, and the genes determine our physical make-up. And there are also some effects on our lives from the political, social, and economic environment – but it is not of all that great a consequence. Einstein would still have been essentially Einstein, and Darwin would still have been interested in natural sciences, no matter what the circumstances, no matter what country they were born in.

But even the genes are not all-powerful, as thought by some scientists. Ever since their discovery scientists have ascribed the evolution of species to the completely random and haphazard mutation of these genes, but they did not have the slightest idea of just what caused these mutations. They still don't! For they do not understand the conversation that is going on between the soul and the mind, and between the mind and the body. There is little evidence of any trans mission of the talents of Einstein, Darwin, Dickens, or Tennyson in succeeding generations. There are no long lines or issue of little Einsteins running around. Hitler was captivated by

Wagner's opera cycle The Ring of the Nibelungs, and thought he could build a master race – but he was badly mistaken.

The sparrow has a weak body and small wings, and flutters not far; the seagull soars aloft with widespread wings and exalts in its strength, and shrieks its domination. Should the sparrow feel dejected for its lowly status? Should the seagull feel its pride? Should the crippled in body or mind be despised for their infirmities? All these things were ordained by Nature through the genes. The function of the genes is to transmit development information to the growing organism, and to perpetuate the species. The genes can be modified, this modification being normally carried out by Nature, and thus enabling all species and life as a whole to evolve. They are not random mutations.

In this chapter or chamber we will enquire as to what Nature is. The genes have been around for a long time, 'the very hairs of your head are all numbered.' (Matthew 10: 30). Just because somebody in the 20th century gave them a name does not mean that they are to be exalted. There is something in man much greater than genes.

The real debate should be on the relative inputs of the genes, and the *mind* of man. It would be instructive here to delve into the development of the emotions, to ask what is the Will, and what is the connection between them. Also to explore the intensity of emotion, particularly sadness and grief. The individual wishes, decides, and wills the emotion, usually without realising it, for it occurs at the subconscious level. We in our response to the environment, are therefore responsible, no one else.

The thesis would be: The intensity of emotion depends on *will*. Or it maybe, as in Japanese culture, that grief and sadness are due to lack of moral strength; we should then seek to know what moral strength is. Will is of the outer self, moral strength is of the inner self.

There is also a third input, recognised by C. G. Jung; the subconscious mind and the prompting of the inner self. This may as yet be only in a nascent state in man's development, or lying dormant. The mystic is interested in something much more important than the genes; he is interested in the very soul of man.

The soul is caged in by the human body, and also by the human mind, but a moral victory enlivens it and enables it to share in the joy of the united self, when for a brief time the objective self and the inner self feel as one. Alas such moments are rare, for are we not much more likely to fail the test. Each act of love also has this effect. That is why love is so important to us, yet we fail to realise its importance and its power and its peace.

WHO OR WHAT IS GOD?

Dare we ask this question? The question of just what is God has been shied away from, even by the various religions purported to worship him, for too long. Some will say he is beyond human comprehension, and it is not for us to know. But that is avoiding the issue, for actually God is just a human concept or construct, and if we face the question instead of trying to avoid it, many things may well become clearer.

It is a question that needs to be openly discussed, especially in the light of our more advanced understanding of the universe, mainly due to scientific progress in astronomy.

When man first tried to fathom out the world in which he lived he observed many forces beyond his control – thunderstorms, volcanoes, earthquakes, and pestilence to name just a few – and he ascribed them to the gods. Priesthoods arose to appease the gods on behalf of the populace, and the priests were held in awe. Kings, political leaders, and religious authorities have vied for power ever since.

Modem science has tried to free the human mind from these tyrants by simply concentrating on the search for truth without bias, and is to be applauded for this approach. Science does not accept God into the equation, but by looking at the particulars science may not always see the wood for the trees. Nor can it ever know the whole truth, but only gradually approach it from without, for it concerns itself only with the external physical material universe. Some branches of science do try to explore the mind, but they consider it as all contained in the physical brain and its neuronal pathways.

MAN, GOD, AND NATURE
Man's puny attempts to interpret the soul's aspiration to have contact with God may lead to the establishment of organised religions, but these then become prone to misinterpretation, bias, and human error.

God does not have a religion, and he is hardly likely to be interested in any one religion – that is just something for silly humans to fight over. And contrary to what they may claim, priests, archbishops, and popes do not have any privileged access or private channel to God. Indeed the God of religions very probably does not exist. Nor does their heaven exist. Think deeply for yourself about these things. Has anybody ever seen a separate being or entity called God? Has anyone ever returned from heaven and given a detailed and accurate description of such a place? What does exist is the Life-force, the Soul of the universe.

It is surely much more mentally mature and sensible to discover the secrets of nature through scientific research and endeavour, for only nature exists, a life-force as vast as the universe, and existing in the smallest particle; a vital life-force existing in every cell, giving it consciousness.

Nature is completely impersonal. Nature just IS! Nature is the part of God that rules the physical universe. Everyone and everything is equal in the eyes of God, and he has no favourites, and this concurs with the scientific view of the world. But everyone and everything is also special in the eyes of God. This is not just because it was all created by God, but because it IS God. We are all part of nature, and all is one. This Oneness of all, revealed by our looking at the question What is God? is now recognised even by science. For God is the God of all, in whose sight everyone is equal, all life is equal, every particle and atom is of equal importance, all is ONE. This Oneness is in the All and the Nothing, and it is eternal, beyond time and space. To the scientist this is the energy of the big bang, but to the mystic it is the eternal now, the eternal existence, the I AM.

Most people's concept of God is rather vague and

nebulous, and it varies from person to person. It can be said then to be of a personal nature, and evolves as the person evolves. This personal concept is accordingly difficult to define. However, if we take a non-personal more general view we can arrive at a modern and more scientific conception of God, and take this as our definition:

It is the energy of the universe, and its creative power or life-force.

However, to save space and constant repetition, I will continue to use the term God throughout this little treatise, as it is brief and understandable to most people. To the mystic God is infinite, omnipresent, and eternal; but God is not a person, not even a being: God IS Being.

Actually this is not a complete definition of God, for I do not presume to be able to do that. It is a definition of nature, which is the part of God that rules the physical universe. It is a sufficient definition as far as we and this physical universe are concerned. The true answers to what is nature, what is the soul, what is God come only with enlightenment, which we will deal with later.

God IS. He created the physical universe, his son. Perhaps this was to reflect and recognise himself. The creation of the universe established a third state, the interaction between God and the universe – LIFE. Or we may term it the Holy Ghost. The Holy Ghost is the Spirit, the Life, the Word of God, that animates all things. It is the Soul of all things. A part of God called Nature rules the physical universe; Nature the giver, protector and maintainer of Life.

Who or what created you? Your parents, you might suggest. But your parents merely cohabited together, which did not take very much time or effort. Who is the greatest chemist, the greatest biologist, and the greatest physicist ever known? Nature. It was a force, the life-force we call Nature that created you. And as far as this planet is concerned it has been going about its business for the past 4000 million years. It has taken Nature about 80 million years to develop the animal body from primitive shrews to monkeys, and then another seven and a half million years to primitive man. Now that's what you call painstaking effort! Science is our endeavour to understand Nature.

In our night sky countless little stars twinkle. They seemed to be of little use, except perhaps to delight the eye of lovers or amateur astronomers. But they are now known to be absolutely essential for without them there would be no light, no warmth, and no life. They are indeed the lamps of God. How a sun can burn for 5000 million years with little change is truly astounding. Most human beings accept this as just another fact of life, which absolves them from thinking about it overmuch, like unto all the other wondrous facts of life – the wonderful array and properties of the chemical elements produced originally from just the basic hydrogen atom; the creation of the magical liquid water from two gases; the rain, rivers and seas, the moon and tides, the air we breathe, the earth and its produce, the development and proliferation of life-forms, the human brain and mental comprehension. There is a life-force we call Nature that has created and is creating all this. It is in every atom and every cell, everywhere. This life-force is eternal, and periodically renews itself in the physical world through the 'big bang.'

To a mystic everything that exists is holy, for all was made by God, everything contains God in its heart, and all is God. God is life itself. Whatever one wishes to call this life-force, this energy, there is a great mystery here. If a scientist tells you he has solved this mystery do not believe him. Only the soul of a mystic can can feel or sense this divine mystery, and only Sophia could reveal it to you. Jesus explained it thus: 'Which of you if his son asks for bread, will give him a stone? If you then, though you are evil, know how to give good gifts to your children, how much more will your Father in heaven give the Holy Spirit and good gifts to those who ask him?' He is saying that God is like a good, giving, and loving Father. This is the mystery. Certainly science can never quite come to understand and fathom this mystery.

A mystic does not believe, as a follower of religion would, or conjecture as a scientist would; he knows with an inner certainty, and if he does not yet know the answer he will openly admit so. A mystic seeks for the meaning of life, to know oneself, to find and look into one's soul. What lies behind the appearance of things? What is fleeting, what is real and permanent, who or what created the universe? So the scientist and the mystic have the same goals, allowing for different terminologies. The scientist seeks the answers from without, in the external world; the mystic from within. Unlike science, however, mysticism is not a profession. It is not something you choose to be or to do, rather it chooses you – *when you are ready*. Nor do you have to be intellectually clever to be a mystic. The mystic is on a path, and to be clever would be a hindrance on that path.

CHAPTER 5

LIFE AND DEATH

Letters have come to me asking such questions as 'Is there life after death? 'Are we born again?' But the most frequent question is 'Dear Alan, will I see my loved ones again?' This is often because of unresolved issues and sudden sad partings on the loss of a loved one. This tugs at the heartstrings, the more so because the answer is No!

We do have a developing soul personality, or awareness of the soul, but the body and brain of this life are gone forever. All is change. We can never be the same again.

> 'Wouldst that I had shown you a little more love
> Whilst you were still alive.'

It has sometimes been implied in this treatise that we have many lives. But if that is so, why do we not remember our past life or lives? Because we did not have a past life. At birth we have a new brain, with a new physical consciousness, and a new combination of genes; in fact we of course are a new being. The 'we' in this context is the ego, the outer self. The only part of us that is eternal is the soul, which does not have a brain or physical consciousness. Whether or not we become aware of the soul, and to what degree, depends on how we unite our outer and inner selves. As far as the ego is concerned, this brain and this present consciousness, death is the end, the final curtain. Nothing survives death except the soul, and perhaps the non-physical sub-consciousness (see The Attributes of Sophia in The Final Chapter).

The genes and the body are given to you at birth but they are not the real you, they are loaned to you for this one lifetime. If you think about it, this is only right and just. Your soul would not wish to be trapped in this one particular body, this one particular character, this particular way of life for ever. Of course you could say that the outer self of most people would not want to live for too long either. But we usually find that the more egotistical a person is the more he wants to cling on to life and power.

They will resort to any subterfuge to thwart the desire of others for change for the better. The body cannot live for ever, that is not the way that Nature works, and Nature is the master. Everything is governed by the parameters or fundamental constants of this particular universe we live in, inherited at its creation. The longevity of each species is governed by chemical and physical laws, biological processes, and by information transmitted through the genes. Health standards and healthcare will of course improve, and more importantly evolution will still go forward; mankind has only been around for about two and a half million years so he has a long way still to go. Eventually most humans will live to an age of about 140.

Many thousands have turned to so-called psychic mediums to try to contact their loved ones after death, but they do not succeed. Let us consider what happens at death. The brain is lifeless, and together with the body soon decays, eaten by bacteria, worms, and other organisms, and a skeleton of bones remains. The complex molecules of the body break down into simpler molecules, including carbon dioxide and water. These pass into the atmosphere and seep into the ground, some passing into insect life; they pass into rivers, seas, and rain, and pass into plant life and then animal life. All is change. Therefore no physical being is left, nor is there a brain with which to think, or receive sensory stimuli, and so that is the end of the organism. It is not surprising therefore that no contact can be made with the dead, except by so-called mediums and charlatans. 'Flesh and blood cannot inherit the kingdom of God.' (1 Corinthians 15:50).

The only thing that might survive after death would be the immaterial soul. But what is the soul?

1. It is not material, and cannot be affected by the physical world.
2. It is in everyone, like a continuous stream, and makes us all one and all equal.

There are a number of reasons why we like to think there might be life after death:

1. The inequalities, sufferings and tragedies might be somehow karmically resolved.
2. The hope that we may see our loved ones again.

3. The fear of the unknown and finality of death.
4. It pleases our vanity to think we can survive death.

The last two reasons belong to the ego and are not valid, and the second reason is a natural human instinct, but of little or no significance in the universal or cosmic scheme of things. The ego certainly does not survive; the individual character you knew is no more. But do not be too concerned – for it is not the real you; the real you is the subconscious self, the soul personality, which may be born again. The soul itself does live on, because it is an eternal part of the Universal Soul, the immaterial that is, beyond time and space, that created and exists in all things.

We, as individuals, have a soul personality which has been built from the trials of life on this earth. It is our awareness of the soul. In some the awareness is weak, poorly developed; and some may once have been aware but have since lost that awareness, and we speak of them as having lost their souls, their humanity. It is as we become more aware, as we become more one with the soul within, that the eternal reality is revealed to us. Becoming aware of your soul is to take the mystic path. The mystic path is long and arduous, and there will be periods of black despair and doubt, yet it is also beautiful and precious, very few take it, or take only a few steps on it. It is noble, loving, pure in heart, and unsullied by the outer world. O God of my heart, what sublime and exquisite joy comes with this realisation.

It should perhaps be stated here that the genes do

live on, in slightly altered form, but only in the sense that they are transmitted from generation to generation through offspring. Nature causes the individuals of the species to compete for producing offspring in order to better ensure survival of the species. And of course that is why she has made the urge for mating so imperative in the first place! Ah, you casanovas and romeos, you donjuans and libertines, you are really only slaves to the whims of Nature!

If you wish to determine the truth of anything, after debating the pros and cons, refer the matter to your conscience. Always let your conscience be your guide! One may forget the conscience, or come to ignore it, but it is there, and always will be there. Some psychologists have tried to deny it, regarding it as just another fleeting mental state, but then they have not found Truth. Psychology is still only an infant science. But why talk about such a trifling subject here? Is yours truly being naive again, or in his second childhood?

No! It is of the utmost importance to the mystic. The conscience is the final arbiter, our judge and jury. In the end we are all judged – by ourselves. In the rush of life, or the pursuit of gain, many come to forget they have a conscience. But that is why the mystic path is closed to them.

CHAPTER 6

DAWNING REALISATION

Her black dress, so much like unto a nun's habit, made her skin seem white and pure, and a calm strength and power shone from her eyes. The power was in her purity, and purity was in her strength and beauty, so that she could not be withstood. I had somehow seen her when I was a child, and had regarded her as my guardian angel, but was dismayed by such strength. Now after many years something drew me on to try to find her again. But where, and how? I had travelled to various shrines abroad, in Bulgaria, Czechoslovakia and Hungary, but without success.

Sometimes I had dreamt of her. One night in my dream she came up out of a lake, brandishing a sword that gleamed like burnished gold, and power was in that sword to vanquish all enemies. But it was not to be used in a warlike way; it was not to be given to me or to mortal men who would misuse it. She was the goddess of Peace. It was a symbol of strength, but strength in purity and goodness. O, how wonderful and divine she was! No words could describe her.

Then musing one day I realised she was a spiritual

being, and could only be sensed within one's soul. And it was then that she appeared. An exquisitely beautiful red rose unfolded in my mind, and I knew that I was in the presence of SOPHIA.

'You have come to me of your own accord, so I see that you are ready,' her words came to me.

'I love and respect you, and wish to stand up and be counted,' I replied, abashed by my own temerity and purpose.

A great knowledge and wisdom shone in her eyes, and one intuitively felt that she saw behind the appearance of things and people straight into their inner reality. She took my hand and led me to a portal marked "LIFE", and it opened before her presence. And now her words came into my mind: 'Enter here, and when you come out of this chamber tell me what you have experienced.'

Sophia, Queen of my soul, how long have I searched
     for thee
And all the time you were within
For without you I would not even exist.
Life is a gift from thee, and men do not realise it.
You are at the centre of all things, and sustain them
And without you nothing would exist.

I crossed the threshold with initial hope and optimism. I was in a small room, and there was a chair set before a table on which was a large mirror, and I realised that I was meant to sit there. I looked into the mirror and saw a dark and distorted face looking back at me, and I began to feel my unworthiness. I saw my past incarnations with their sins and errors, their bestial ignorance. And I was plunged into a pit of darkness and despair. I could not go on, and stayed there for some time. But then a door opened and rays of light came through it. I had started on this path and must see it through; I arose and went through the door.

And in this chamber I had a dream. Weirdly, I was a new-born child. I opened my eyes but did not see, or comprehend. All was a strange blur, and I cried. I cried to be comforted, to be warmed, to be fed. There was an alien world out there that I had gradually to come to terms with; although my outer self adapted as everyone must if they are to survive I was never really at one with this outer world.

'Why have you sent me here?'

'You will come to realise in time.'

Then I awoke from the dream, but there was a voice still speaking inside my head that said: 'Behold I give you life, and the choice to use it as you will.' Then other thoughts came into my mind. The soul cannot ascend into the higher realms of heaven without the guide of an angel. As the soul ascends the light brightens and shines more and more. The angels, or souls in the heavens, live in a greater light than we who live on this earth. We are in darkness, firstly because the material realm is further away from God, but this is not of our doing. However, the second reason is of our doing, and this is the darkness of selfhood, of pride, vanity, and egotism. Which leads ever downwards, to greed, fear, hate, envy, lust and depravity. O, if you would only see yourself.

The mental state is not fixed as we jump from one

emotion to another; indeed psychiatrists may alter the mental state in order to combat neuroses or phobias. This fact could lead one to jump to the conclusion that we ourselves are just creatures of the whims of the moment with no permanency or real self. And as many have declared after the discovery of our genetic make-up, that we are not responsible for our actions. But this is not so. If you really study a human child's development you will find that besides the gradual learning of the environment and development of the brain's 'clean slate', there is an underlying personality already there. Scientists will no doubt ascribe this to the inherited genes, but to the mystic it is not so. There is a soul in every human being above and beyond and greater than any gene. Do you not sense it so, do you not feel it so? You know that it is so. You know that you are responsible for your own actions.

There are no sudden cut-offs or compartments in the Oneness of Creation. We compartmentalise things and areas in order to grapple with them more easily. But these compartments do not exist in reality. As Darwin realised everything in nature follows a gradual progression or evolution. Therefore to say that Life began with the first cell or amoeba is a miscomprehension. Life began at the creation of the universe, or perhaps even before. At the 'big bang', or the explosion of energy out of the Nothing, life was already in the energy, and by the means of number matter was born. Every particle, every atom is alive with this energy. Plant and animal life is a natural progression of this energy.

The electrons revolve around the nucleus which vibrates with energy, the moons and planets revolve around the suns which vibrate with energy, the cells are vibrating; all is in ceaseless motion. If the motion stopped nothing would exist! God is the father, the universe is His son, and the motion is the Holy Spirit, the Holy Ghost, the voice of God, the music of the spheres, the Word. This cannot be sensed by the outer eyes and ears, but only by the inner senses of the soul.

Mind has found its home in many kinds, and we are part of the many kinds and they of us. We are privileged to share in this panorama of nature and its energy, and to use it. But it is not ours, it is much greater than we are, infinitely greater – and holy. Every fly, beetle, tiger, human, or blade of grass is holy. To take another person's life is like unto taking your own.

O Nature, thou art resplendent
I bow my head in humility before thee.

Our mortal life has a birth and a death. This must be so, or we would think we were as gods. We would be a thousand times more egotistical and wicked than we are now. But the real life, God's life, is eternal, without beginning or end. Sophia's words came into my mind, words I remembered from previous encounters with her, although at that time I had not grasped their significance.

- - - - -*my purpose is to give you life*
                    - - - - -*do you not realise this is so*
- - - - -*some day you will know*
          - - - - -*and you will not fear me as you do now*
- - - - -*one day perhaps you will come to me, and love me*

Then I came to a fork in the Path. One road was broad and easy to walk along, and also enticing with thousands of alluring objects on either hand, and many were taking it – so surely it must be the one to follow, with treasures galore to fill our pockets with. It would be best to join the throng and grab my share before all these others plundered it. Anyway the other path looked narrow and rather bare, and it was awkward to squeeze through the gate. But I hesitated, and sat down to think, for I was troubled and in a quandary. Meditating long and hard, I waited for the still small voice of my conscience to answer. Finally I took the narrow path that was on the right-hand fork, but was still not sure if I had chosen aright, for the path I had chosen seemed to be leading me out into the open.

PART FOUR

LIGHT
Not by Bread Alone

CHAPTER 7

THE LIGHT OF UNDERSTANDING

When one breaks down the whole into its constituent parts, usually in order to simplify things and provide an explanation, anomalies and contradictions arise. This happens to the scientist when they break down the atom into its constituent particles and lose sight of the whole, and it happens in all other areas too, even in the pursuit of mysticism. This is because the whole becomes lost in the forest of particulars, whereas only the whole exists – the particulars, or indeed the particles, do not exist in nature on their own. All is one. The first mystic law is All is One. It should always be in our thoughts. This is why real understanding comes only with the flash of illumination when the consciousness becomes absorbed into the whole. It is why the mystic path cannot be travelled for you.

At the exit of the first chamber Sophia was waiting for me with outstretched hands, and smiling in welcome.

"Come and rejoice, for you have passed the first test."

"I did not know that I was being tested," I replied.

"Life is one long test. When we overcome one obstacle we are then prepared and ready for the next."

Strength and life radiated from her, yet behind it was also joy, even a sense of humour. And we stood before a second portal marked 'LIGHT.'

Again it opened at her mere presence.

"Enter here, and when you come out tell me what you have understood."

I entered, and these thoughts came into my mind. It is only as we travel the mystic path and become aware, that the Light comes in, and we attain a spiritual life, the Greater Life. To travel the mystic path is to gradually become more one with the soul within. Mystics seek and yearn for the day when the light of understanding will flood in, when for a brief instant they are one with the Eternal. It occurs at a point when the selfhood is finally vanquished and surrenders at last to be one with the soul. This influx of understanding is known as Enlightenment or Nirvana.

One of the first lessons to learn on the path is humility. This does not mean to abase oneself, to be servile, to grovel to others, but to have overcome the pride of the ego.

Only the humble of heart may approach God.

CHAPTER 8

ILLUMINATION

The Roman statesman and scholar, and later emperor, Marcus Aurelius was born in 121 AD, and had remarkable insights of wisdom for his era. We can see examples of this in the following words:

#Whatever the world may say or do, my part is to keep myself good; just as a gold piece, or an emerald, or a purple robe insists perpetually "Whatever the world may say or do, my part is to remain a gold piece, an emerald, or a purple robe and keep my colour true."

#Cast no side-glance at the instincts governing other men. Let reason be your helmsman. The senses should be subservient to the mind.

#Take it that you have died today, and your life's story is ended; and henceforward regard what further time may be given you as an uncovenanted bonus, and live it out in harmony with nature.

#Dig within. There lies the wellspring of good; ever dig, and it will ever flow.

#Live out your days in untroubled serenity, refusing to be coerced, though the whole world deafen you with its demands.

#Even the Sun-god himself will tell you, "There is a work that I am here to do", and so will all the other sky-dwellers. For what task, then, were you yourself created?

The roman catholic and Trappist monk Thomas Merton (1915–1968) took the mystical path of meditation, revealing the insights that he received in the book *Seeds of Contemplation*.

The clearest examples of enlightenment are however provided by the Buddha, and Jesus of Nazareth.

The essence of Buddhism is that we all have the potential to be enlightened if we overcome the false ego, and enter into the silence, the emptiness and stillness of the present moment. The teachings are transmitted from master to student verbally and by example rather than written down.

There have been Buddhas in earlier times and more will appear in the future. The last incarnation of the Buddha is said to have been Siddhartha Gautama, son of a king, born in 563 BC. About six years after he left the palace where he had lived in sensuous luxury for the first thirty years of his life and began his spiritual journey, he had an awakening, the influx of nirvana, when 'he saw with new eyes'. He had a realisation of freedom from self, from attachment to the world, from suffering. It should be noted that Siddhartha was just a normal human being until he became imbued with the spirit of the Buddha, and he became a Teacher. The Buddha asks us to renounce the original sin of egotism and return our consciousness back into the soul. To discard the turmoil and vacillations of the outer consciousness and its conditioning, and retreat back into the inner silence from whence all came, to free oneself from the tyranny of the outer self, the ego, and be absorbed back into the Infinite, the Oneness. The Buddha tells us that we are all subject to the Wheel of Life and Death until all karma has been resolved, and at the last we become one with the Infinite.

In these days of wider dissemination of knowledge many of the teachings or sutras of the Buddha have become written down, and we may perhaps reflect on a few extracts here.

#Avoiding extremes the Middle Path is the Noble Eightfold Path, namely right view, right thought, right speech, right action, right livelihood, right effort, right mindfulness, right concentration.

#Let one cultivate a boundless heart towards all beings. Let one's thoughts of boundless love pervade the whole world.

#Even as solid rock is unshaken by the wind, so are the wise unshaken by praise or blame.

#He whose senses are mastered like horses well under the charioteer's control, he who is purged of pride, free from passions, such a steadfast one even the gods envy.

#Being dispassionate he becomes detached; through detachment he is liberated.

#Calm is the thought, calm the word and deed of him who, rightly knowing, is wholly freed, perfectly peaceful and equipoised.

#One may conquer in battle a thousand times a

thousand men, yet he is the best of conquerors who conquers himself.

#Not to do any evil, to cultivate good, to purify one's mind, this is the Teaching of the Buddha.

#The conqueror begets enmity; the defeated lie down in distress. The peaceful rest in happiness, giving up both victory and defeat.

According to some mystical teachings Satan is the prevailing power in this world, the prince of this world, who fills our minds with his multiplicity. All souls in this world are the slaves of Satan and our minds are entangled in his web. We are in the prison of this world and of the body, until we have paid all our debts. Everything, good or bad, great or small, even a thought has its consequences, and is subject to the law of Karma. We can often see this process of cause and effect in the lives of others, how they are responsible for the events which overtake them, but we do not see it in ourselves. Only the Truth coming from an enlightened teacher such as Jesus or the Buddha can set the soul free. Like all things Satan was created by God and has an important role to play in the scheme of things. He is resident in our restless vacillating minds, and to bind him we must first learn to control the mind.

Jesus, of course, was just a normal human being born of Mary and Joseph. Then at his illumination at the age of 32 he was imbued with the Christ Spirit, which brings oneness with God, and he became a Teacher. Jesus teaches us how to conduct ourselves in this life, and how to live with and behave to one another. Jesus also proclaims the Kingdom of Heaven, and the mystical divinity of all creation and of mankind. Contrary to perceived opinion he did not establish a religion; the religion was established later by Rome. The State, or the ruling dynasties, realised early on in the development of civilisation that they needed to embrace religion as an aid in controlling the populace. But Jesus said this: 'When you pray, enter into your closet, and when thou hast shut the door pray to your Father in secret, and thy Father who seeth in secret shall reward thee openly.' (Matthew 6:6).

In the story of Jesus, as with all historical events, some things strike the logical reasoner as embellishments added after the event, whereas other things strike one as undoubtedly true. Always refer the matter to your conscience, your inner self. Virgin birth, resurrection, and miracles were expected and required attributes of any avatar or messianic figure, when being advocated by religious authorities or rulers. Miracles in the accepted or religious sense do not happen – except that every day is a miracle, and that the whole of life is a wonderful miracle. And the wonders of science are not really the wonders of science; they are the wonders of Nature, for science merely discovers or uncovers these wonders, and man may research and manipulate them for his own purposes. Jesus had brethren, and it is thought he had three brothers the eldest of which was James, who was also known as Joseph of Arithmathea. He may also have had a wife although there is no proof of this; certainly Mary Magdalene was a close disciple. As mentioned in chapter 3 the religious authorities deleted most of the writings about her because they were opposed to the veneration of women.

All the above comments do not detract from the words of Jesus, which are the words of Truth inspired in him by the Holy Ghost. From the moment of his enlightenment or descent of the Holy Ghost, Jesus stated with absolute confidence and certainty 'Heaven and earth shall pass away, but my words shall not pass away.' 'And lo, I am with you always, even unto the end of the world.' Many of the words of Jesus are of course recorded by his apostles, and should be diligently studied. The correct procedure for the student of mysticism is to read only one parable or one small section at a time. and meditate upon it for at least a day or longer, especially in the evening before retiring. Only then proceed to the next section.

Let us now look, while we are in this chamber of Light, at just one phrase: *Blessed are the meek. for they shall inherit the earth*. How can that be so? What does it really mean? Then move from the outer thoughts to the stillness and peace of the inner self. and meditate. Do not be too disappointed if you receive no answers, or if the phrase still means little to you, for a mystic may spend a year contemplating just a few words before the full import of the truths they contain become a part of the inner self. But above all the mystic way has to be lived and experienced. not just comprehended intellectually.

Lain buried in the sands since biblical times, a batch of papyrus scrolls in book form hidden in an earthenware jar was discovered in 1945 amongst which was the Gospel of Thomas. The essential message of this gospel is that one must overcome or transcend the objective egoistic self, and find the real self within. One of the verses of this gospel may instruct us here, at this stage on the path.

#His disciples said to him: On which day will the Kingdom come? Jesus answered: It will not come by expectation. They will not say: "Behold, it is here!" or "Behold, there!" But the Kingdom of the Father is spread out over the earth and men do not see it.

Heaven is here and now. but men in their selfhood do not see it.

The teachings of Jesus and those of the mystic path are sometimes veiled in metaphor and parables, and here is the key.

Ascension, resurrection: terms for the spiritual ascent of the soul.

Bread, manna: spiritual wisdom of the Word.

Darkness: immersion in this world.

The Devil, devils: the ego.

Enemies, tares: human weaknesses.

Fisher-kings; the apostles, and those of the lineage of Jesus.

Green pastures: mansions of the soul. Harvest: the fruits of spiritual endeavours. Mountains; inner realms of the spirit.

Raising of the dead: spiritual awakening. To be raised from the dead is not a physical raising, but a spiritual one. It is to be saved from egotism and immersion in this world, and to be restored into the Book of Life.

Ship, ferryboat, barge: the guiding hand of Jesus,or the soul which can take us through the turbulent waves of the mind to the land of light.

Strong man: Satan.

The Word: God's spirit and wisdom. God's creative power and glory.

Valley of the shadow of death: this world.

The holy communion or eucharist: The blessing of bread and wine was a common and widespread practice from earliest times, even among pagan Romans. The observance of this ritual by modern Christians may be helpful to the soul however – *if* it is observed in the correct manner, that is in a reverent mood and with sincere motivation, which brings the image of Jesus before us and in our hearts.

Satan is necessary so that we may learn, so that we can overcome and aspire to better things, so that we can see and know we have a purpose.

A STRANGE MYSTIC PHILOSOPHY

If everything came out of the Nothing, perhaps we are living in a dream, God's dream. If he stopped dreaming of us we would be no more. Perhaps he has countless dreams. This seems far-fetched, but it is certainly true that all things arise from thoughts and ideas,, archetypes in the mind and consciousness. It may be that the dream is not directly from God, but from ourselves. We may be living in our own dream, and that whatsoever we think about and envisage will come to pass. The thoughts we have then assume vital significance to our very survival. Every little seemingly trivial thought, good or had, is thwart with karmic consequences. On this philosophy it is vital that we learn to control our minds and thoughts. Every thought of anger and hate will beget anger and hate. Every thought of kindness and love will beget kindness and love.

THUS SPAKE ZARATHUSHTRA

Most of the teachings of Zoroaster have been lost or destroyed. The hymns of Zoroaster, known as the *Gathas*, remain together with other liturgies and prayers, and many of the teachings show parallels to those of Christianity, particularly as regards the book of Revelation. Zoroaster lived in Persia, and became a seer or prophet. He is thought to have lived many centuries before Christ at around 1250 BC, and his teachings have high ethical standards. Meditating on the problem of good and evil Zoroaster began to experience divine revelations. Ahura Mazda, the one god, was dual in nature, both good and evil. To overcome evil Ahura Mazda made the world, as a battleground where the two forces would meet, and the triumph of good over evil would be accomplished by the holy spirit.

Zoroastrians worship the one god Ahura Mazda, Lord of Wisdom, and under him Mithra and Varuna, who are Lords of the covenant and oath, which bind men together. As long as mankind worships these gods the world will endure, governed by the principle of Asha, the life force. As in most ancient religions it is believed that ritual sacrifices were once used to propitiate the gods. Fire is present in all creations as a hidden life force. It also represents truth and righteousness, and their places of worship are called fire temples. The sacred fire is kept burning atop a pillar, usually in a metal vessel. As in other religions light symbolises good, and darkness is evil. A flame is never blown out, but allowed to die down naturally. Zoroastrians maintain high standards of cleanliness, believing cleanliness is next to godliness, and they have a number of purification rites, often using the burning of incense.

The ultimate aim of the virtuous striving to overcome evil is to bring about the kingdom of Ahura Mazda on earth. *The flame of Zoroaster is not extinguished, and it will shine once more upon the world.*

I come to you again to light the eternal flame of truth in your hearts. And Ahura Mazda says this to me:

Do not believe in the previous false gods, nor in the after false gods – only Ahura Mazda exists. Only Ahura Mazda exists, nothing else exists, for all is contained and lives in him. Do not put your hope in some future time and place. That future time and place does not exist, only the now exists. Immerse yourself in the present moment, for this is all that can be said to really exist. And it does contain *All*, if you will open your inward eye and see it. It is endless and infinite, if you will open your inward sense and feel it. It is the real unconscious world of the soul and of God, filled with calmness and peace. And you know that hatred does not exist here, do you not?

If there is any hatred in your heart, and you think that you are on the right path to heaven, then you are deceived, for there is no hatred in heaven. Cleanse your mind therefore from the evils of envy and hate, for it is now in this present moment, that holiness and love must prevail and be experienced, not in some future time and place. Aspire to my purity and holiness, the stillness and calm of my truth. In my purity is strength and love. Under my protecting wing, let it grow in your heart, and it will force out all evil thought. The ego will be forgotten, and you will be born again into the miracle of my life.

CHAPTER 9

FOR JUST THIS MOMENT

What is the soul? What is nature? We may as well ask: What is God? The answers to these questions come only with enlightenment, the influx of nirvana. In enlightenment we connect with the over-soul, the universal or cosmic consciousness that is the source of all things. We may term it God, or Nature, the inner self of all things. Enlightenment thus occurs when the inner self and the outer self become one. It may be but for a moment. If it occurred completely and permanently one would indeed have eternal life.

It must be emphasised however, that the majority of mankind is trapped in the outer self, the ego. The mystic path is a closed book to them. For as Thomas a' Kempis has said "it is because men do not understand that they must utterly renounce their own will, that so few become enlightened and enjoy inward liberty." It is perhaps here that it may be remarked that just one individual is worth a thousand communist states – for he has a soul. The mystic path is precious and beautiful, but open only to the meek in heart, in peace and love and purity.

Do not despair of mankind, however! Not everyone can be a Buddha or would want to be one. Most of us still manage to evolve and take a few steps along the path, without our conscious knowledge and in spite of ourselves. This comes about when we quieten the ego for a while, and dream or meditate, either consciously or unconsciously while we sleep. Also lessons are learned the hard way – through the trials and tribulations of this earthly life.

Some systems would negate the body, the senses, the outer self entirely, but they are in error. For the physical world and the body are also divine, but you did not realise this before, not in the correct manner, before you liberated the soul, before you restored the divine self to its rightful place as Ruler.

What lessons had I learned on the Path so far?

To be at one with the soul, and to be guided by her. To be patient, tolerant, gentle.

To meet every event with equanimity, detachment, and innocent goodwill. To be pure and noble, in thought, word, and deed.

And that any man is strong whose heart is pure.

And what could I tell Sophia that I now understood?

The first step on the path is to realise that one does have a soul. The second, to realise that this soul is the real important part of you, and not the changing ego. The third, to restore the soul to its rightful place. To disentangle oneself from the world and the ego. To be a part of it, but not of it. To be free from it, not immersed in it. When one empties the mind of the false ego it then needs filling with spiritual thoughts and the Word. For beware, one needs to be vigilant, for the enemy that is the ego, will surely try to get back in, and if he has an empty mind to fill he will be stronger than ever.

God is not a person, he is not some being up in the heavens, he is not some outside power or force, he is not even a Creator.

He *is* the universe, he *is* nature, he *is* light, he *is* love, he *is* life itself. Short simple words, but they have a profound meaning behind them.

Contemplation of beauty can be a help to us on the path. For instance, a painting, a poem, a symphony, a walk in the woods, a glorious sunset. Where there is spiritual expression through music, painting, and poetry we can be moved with their beauty. They have a spiritual power that awakens what is already resident in our souls. Once we start on the path we find our tastes and likings change for the better, and we move towards higher beautiful things.

But now let us wait here for a while.

For we cannot go on without Sophia's permission. And we must rest, for the journey is not all plain sailing, there will be setbacks on the way, for we are all full of faults and weaknesses of character. We cannot be illuminated till we have overcome the ego, and cast out our devils.

PART FIVE

LOVE
The Intangible
Mystery

CHAPTER 10

THE FINAL ATTAINMENT

There was this woman sat on a bench in the broad avenue leading to the shopping precinct, an elderly, tired, and sad-looking woman. As I passed her the thought came to me, 'Give her a smile and a friendly word of encouragement.' But as usual I did not react to this thought quickly enough, and carried on walking briskly past, intent only on pursuing my own interests. However, as I was doing my shopping the picture of her face came unbidden into my mind, sad and forlorn, and tugged at my heartstrings. If she is still there I will speak to her on the way back, I said to myself. But when I returned she was no longer there. I never saw her again. The stranger at the gate will only appear once, perhaps thrice in a lifetime. Beware, lest the moment begone.

★★★

At the exit of the second chamber Sophia was not there, and for a while I felt a keen sense of disappointment. I realised that I had further to go, till I did not feel disappointment, only love. I knew she would not come now, until I was tried and ready. The only thing that it was in my power to do was to try to carry on along the path. Even if I finally won through it would only be by the grace of Sophia that the door would be opened to my knock.

One day on the path I had a dream and in this dream I stood at the Gates. On the other side of these Gates riches could be seen, seemingly there for the taking. Yet there was no lock, and as I pressed lightly on the Gate it opened a little space. And I marvelled that vagabonds and thieves passed by and did not enter, whilst it was left so unguarded... yet perhaps there is a guardian at the Gate.

The soul yearns for love, but most human love is rather a restricted thing, and is still part of the ego. For even Hitler and Stalin had their spouses. Of course, it may extend a little to one's children and family. The young child thrives on the love of its parents, and it is a tragedy if it is deprived of that love for some reason. And so it was at this time I began to recall my first and only true love.

Love gives us all a taste of the divine. Any man is rich who has love in his heart, and if it is between soulmates it becomes a truly wondrous thing.

Love was ours, filling the world with its song
The darkest day with its light, right triumphed over
    wrong
And the radiance of your smile proclaimed
That love was ours; yes, love was ours.

And in that precious moment when our hearts
    entwined
I knew it would last forever through all space and time.
I will know you again, my darling; and in some
    future time
When you look at me and I touch you
I will be yours, you will be mine.

This human love is not to be despised or belittled as some religious systems might do. It is in accordance with the design of Nature, and at its highest level of the mind and soul is also divine. If it is merely at the animal level however, then it is just self-gratification, and will hinder you on the path. Human beings have been made higher than animals for they have consciousness of consciousness. This gives us greater choice, but also greater responsibility. Some animals indeed may have better physical bodies than us, but they do not have that consciousness that would enable them to conceive and visualise God, and thus cannot aspire to Him.

But most men do not realise that if the soul were in its rightful position, in charge of the being of man, then love could be greatly extended to all mankind and to God. Blessed are they who seek not self-gratification but to love and be loved, to give and receive, to know and be known, who desire light and truth.

…and love burst forth and could be contained no longer, into the mighty universe, for what could be stronger or more powerful? Perhaps it would be instructive to see what others had to say about love, and what importance they attached to it.

The words of St. John:

"We know that we have passed from death to life, because we love our brothers. Anyone who does not love remains in death".

"God is love. Whoever lives in love lives in God, and God in him".

The words of St. Paul:

"If I speak in the tongues of men and of angels, but have not love, I am only a sounding brass or a clanging cymbal. If I have the gift of prophecy and can fathom all mysteries and all knowledge, and if I have a faith that can move mountains, but hath not love, I am nothing. If I give all I possess to the poor and surrender my body to the flames, but hath not love, I gain nothing. Love is patient, love is kind, it does not envy, it does not boast, it is not proud. It is not rude, it is not self-seeking, it is not easily angered, it keeps no record of wrongs. Love does not delight in evil but rejoices with the truth. It always protects, always trusts, always hopes, always perseveres. Love never fails".

The words of Thomas a' Kempis, a 15th century Augustinian monk, in *The Imitation of Christ* (1424):

"A wonderful thing is love, a mighty good indeed – for love alone makes every burden light, and endures with calmness all the roughness of the world. For it bears a burden without being burdened, and makes all that is bitter, sweet and delicious. Love longs to lift itself on high. Nothing is sweeter than love, nothing stronger,

*nothing loftier, nothing wider, nothing pleasanter,
nothing richer or better, in heaven or earth, because love
is born of God, and can find its rest in God alone, above
all created things".*

Meditating on the words and sayings of other people, even of the great teachers, will not however, of itself, give us entry into the Kingdom. The mystic path is to be lived and experienced by you yourself. One must apply oneself and practise the mystic teachings. One must be a doer of the Word, not just pay lip service, not just understand intellectually. And so we must learn to concentrate and control the mind, and then apply oneself to meditation; to meditate on and in His love, by night and by day. The soul of the mystic yearns to be with God, to be one with God. This yearning has been expressed by Emily Bronte in her poems, particularly in *The Prisoner* and *Last Lines*. We must be instructed by, through, and in the Spirit.

You have to become a Buddha yourself, or one with the Christ within. All the books are nothing, merely a part of the egotism of the world. First learn to feel and have empathy for mankind, the animal kingdom, the whole of nature. Then open your heart to love and humility. Then the path must be travailed, toiled and worked upon; it is a long path to overcome the ego, the outer self, till you knock at the door of the real Self within, God within. It is by no means easy. The ego, for all its bombast, is filled with fear, and these fears beget hatred instead of love. They are our real enemies.

The Kingdom of Heaven is here and now. Christ is within you. 'Lo, I am with you alway, even unto the end

233

of the world.' But although you may stand at the door and knock, it will not open till you are ready. For some will knock and Jesus will say, 'I never knew you.' And so I abided outside the last chamber, which I could see but a short distance away, and I meditated thus:

Perhaps I have gone far enough in this present life. Surely I am not worthy to go any farther on the path. The very fact that I am still using the word 'I', and thinking of myself as I, is a barrier to any further progress. We are all at different stages on the path, and not even the saintliest of us is worthy to approach God. Man is only slightly higher than the animals; indeed he is a greater sinner than many lesser creatures. And then when the door to the soul does ope it will probably be only for brief moments. If it were longer we would surely die in its ecstasy, for like Galahad we would not want to return. There are many stages of development, many mansions to reside in, and it is not surprising there are many barriers.

We must not rush therefore, but learn to be calm and still.

One night I clearly heard her voice calling me, and she said 'Would you rather that you see with your two outer eyes, or the inward spiritual eye? YOU, who stands at the crossroads and waits, choose now the way – the outer ego, or the real inner self.' And then Sophia said this to me: 'Your soul is divine, but you. your ego, is not divine, for I have given you life of your own to use as you will. You must think about this before you can advance further on the Path.

And then later, on another night, I had this dream.

All my kindred and my friends were round my bedside. Also those who had passed on before me: My mother and father and members of my family, my wife and her family, hovering in the background. Perhaps

I am dying, and it is time to go, I thought. But the overriding thought that came to me was how self-centred I had been, being so critical of all those people, friends and others, of judging them thoughtlessly.

For now I saw them with their own burdens and problems; they too were travellers on the path. And I asked Sophia to forgive me.

For a long time my only thought was

'Forgive me, Sophia. Please forgive me.'

'Forgive me, Sophia. Please forgive me.'

It was only then that she came back to me. One day, to my great joy, she came and welcomed me.

'Rejoice, for you have passed the second test.' 'Now I see where your wisdom lies,' I replied.

But my awe of her was greater than ever, for I had a realisation that she was even above and beyond enlightenment. She did not need to be enlightened, for she was enlightenment itself. She looked at me with those penetrating eyes, and smiled. 'Do not be disheartened, for you have further to go on the Path.'

She led me to a third portal, which opened as she approached. "There is now only one more key that you need to open the door that leads to the Kingdom of Heaven. Here I leave you, for when you emerge from here you will be one with me. You will embrace me and love me, love me, love me!!! O, how you will love me! And I will love you in return. You will know where my power lies, and it will not disconcert you as it once did. If you live in me you cannot be afraid – because Nature is not afraid."

And I came into a garden, wherein a magnolia tree grew. It was bare, but each year in the Spring it bloomed again in beauty, and mauve or purplish-pink fluted goblet-like flowers adorned it in glory. It spoke to me, not in words but telepathically, of flowering, of the beauty of the soul. And in the tree sat six blackbirds which looked at me wisely. There were always just six, for when they prospered and were too many they would chase the newcomers off to find other places for themselves. There was no malice in this, it was their instinct of what was best for the continuance of their species, and their wisdom was passed down the generations. They too spoke to me of many things, and in this delight I was entranced and fell into an enchanted sleep. I was transported to a magical island, and on this island there was no time or hurry, only peace and love. And so I abode there.

A calm, profound, and blissful serenity lay on the land, which was bathed in light, and although an island there seemed space for all And when I gazed around me I was in an enchanted land of green pastures, wherein the soul can lie in peace, and be restored in health. Not far off grew shrubs and trees resplendent in their foliage, bearing exquisite flowers and fruits, of which none were too old or too ripe, as if time had come to a stop. I had no hunger for physical food, but of a yearning for spiritual sustenance – for life and joy, for light and wisdom, for love. Yes, for love, sweet mystery of life. Oh, let me stay here, and repose in thee for evermore. It was balm to the soul to be freed for a while from the incessant chunnering of the countless egos in the outer world.

Perhaps it was the isle of Avalon in the Otherworld. For a lady of the spirit came to me with a dove on her shoulder, and bathed me in her Peace. And one like unto Nimue placed her hand on my brow, and healed the sadness of my heart, and gave me hope and strength to carry on. And I was filled with love. Love for them, for they were giving love to me. But I knew they were only messengers, angels who served a higher power, and somehow I knew Sophia was part of this higher power. And although my soul had not ascended very high, I was content with the green valley, and what I had achieved so far.

My soul did not want to leave, but my awakening body tugged me back to the mainland. I too awoke and found myself back under the magnolia tree, but somehow I felt different I perceived the tree and the blackbirds, and they looked back at me – but now I was the tree and the blackbirds; and they were me.

Weights seemed to drop from me, the burden that I had carried all my life seemed to be gone, and I stood up straight and tall, yet calm and peaceful. I felt a new strength in me, and my soul sang 'My strength is as the strength of ten because my heart is pure.' Purity cannot be withstood, all doors must open to it; and love is so gentle, all darkness withers before it. Towards the end of the mystic path mercy and love triumph even over judgement, and all is forgiven. Love is the supreme spiritual and mystical law, the essence of existence, the most dynamic force in the universe, the ultimate rule and guide in everything.

This love is not just for mankind alone. This vast universe was created long before man existed, and Nature has filled it with many treasures which man is privileged to discover and share in, as he slowly advances from primitive ape to a mature mental and spiritual being. There is an unconditional giving in the universe: 'For he maketh His sun to rise on the evil and on the good, and sendeth His rain on the just and the unjust.' The final attainment is to be receptive to this love, and to radiate it outwards to all others, including all animal life. For God has made us the shepherds of the world.

And when I returned from my mystic journey I found myself in another garden, the Garden of Heaven, that I had not seen before, that I had not been aware of. It was not in some remote place, up above the clouds or beyond the stars, nor in some future time, but right here beside me. In this garden love and purity blossomed, because there was no hate there. Peace prevailed and held sway over all. A peace that was deep, profound, and powerful – more powerful than the noise and explosions of war. This was a wonder, a marvellous wonder that filled me with joy. I had come to know on my journey that love was more powerful than hate, but now I began to realise and feel and sense that *Peace* was the victor and the *Ruler*.

You cannot walk in this garden unless and until you have clasped Sophia, told her you love her, and you and Sophia are ONE.

Yes, I now know you Sophia for who and what you are. I love you with a pristine love, for you are Purity itself. Forgive us for our trespasses against you.

I stood naked before her. All my weaknesses, my faults, my sins, and egotism were exposed, and there was no hiding place. But I knew it was time for me to come to her and do this; I had delayed and prevaricated all my life, perhaps for many lives, and she had waited patiently for me to at last come to her and acknowledge her as the real me my soul.

The conceited egotistical stupidity and error of my ways smote me to the heart with remorse. 'Please forgive me,' I simply said, for there was no excuse for my behaviour. Tears welled up in my eyes, tears of remorse. But now I realised they were also mixed with tears of self-pity, so I ceased to cry, and looked at her fully, into those eyes that saw everything and knew everything and for the first time in my life I saw truth and purity.

With reverence I saw their sublime majesty, and knelt before her. And then I sensed these words, as if written in my mind:

"Because you have come to me of your own accord, and have asked nothing for yourself, then you may enter into my kingdom and be one with me."

I realised the absolute immensity of this gift.

The rose unfolded, and pierced my heart with its beauty.
And I was one with Sophia at last.

And then a truth was revealed to me
that I had only vaguely understood before:

There is joy in heaven when just one returns to the fold.

CODA

Do I have to follow the Middle Path, the Eightfold Path, the Four Noble Truths, the Wheel of birth and death?

Do I have to follow the complicated arcane searching for the philosophers stone?

Do I have to follow Sir Galahad and seek for the Holy Grail?

Do I have to delve into the psychology of Jung, and study attitude and functional types, and archetypes, and the eight psychological types, shadows, personas, the animus and anima?

Do I have to follow an organised religion? No! At the present time the majority of mankind still needs an organised religion to guide them, but one day we will outgrow divisive religions, for true religion is within.

We do not have to do any of these things. There are many paths and we are free to choose and make our own path. This book has been about the path to Truth, the mystic path of the soul. Only three keys are required to.open the door: LOVE, NOBILITY, PURITY. They awaken what is already present in the Soul, and the Soul itself will unlock the door and open it to you, making you whole, and giving you its profound peace.

But if we are to renounce the world altogether, why

are we here? One reason could be that through the trials and tribulations of this life we evolve the psyche until it is one with the Soul within. That indeed is the aim of the mystic path. But what then? What is our destiny then? The Buddha seeks only annihilation or absorption into the Infinite, and cessation from earthly life. Man-made religions have only a very nebulous idea of what could lie ahead, and think perhaps we could float about with the angels in heaven.

In truth one day the physical universe will end, and scientists judge that the sun has about 5000 million years to go, the earth somewhat less, and the universe as a whole about twenty billion years. So although it will end it is a very very long time. But time is only relative; time and space do not exist in reality. The earth could end tomorrow, and in a cosmic sense it would hardly matter! One would have to accept it as the luck of the draw. If one has travelled the mystic path he will accept it with equanimity.

However, while we are on this earth we are physical beings with rational minds to think with. Rationally we have a long way to go. On the mystic path we have learnt we are also spiritual beings. So now we can come back to earth, so to speak, with a different perspective, having united the two parts of our being. Now we see that our mission is to live here in this physical universe, that it too is a divine creation. Once we have realised our own divinity we can rejoin the rest of creation reborn with a new spirit, a new vision, without self-egotism. Heaven is not in some future time or in a further space. It is here and now, ifwe seek it and wish to live in it. It is the same with hell. Heaven is of the soul, hell is of the ego. The choice is ours.

> *Thy Kingdom come, Thy will be done on earth,*
> *as it is in heaven.*

AND NOW

And now we must stand up and be counted, for we are going to be called upon to do battle. For we have many enemies, both within and without. Did I not say it would not all be plain-sailing? And now we see why we had to be prepared for so long, before we were ready, or we would fall at the first onslaught. Peace, truth, and purity have many enemies. There are many little hitlers strutting about the world, performing on this stage. They see only themselves, and do not know that they are being watched. But we now know that both they and we are constantly and faithfully watched. We will not fight with swords – for we have learnt that no power on earth is greater than Love.

And all is faithfully recorded. Do not be deceived as Arathain was, for every thought, word, and deed is faithfully written into the Book of Life. All is recorded in the Otherworld, where the thieves of this world cannot get at it, and the Otherworld is not far away. We need just take the ship across the stretch of turbulent sea to the Isle of Avalon. The scientists also will try to get at it, but they will not succeed, for they do not understand. They too are of this world. The Otherworld is immaterial, and to scientists it is insubstantial and non-existent. But yet it is eternal and enduring, from which the material universe sprung. Strangely, it is the seemingly solid universe that is the unsubstantial dream, and teeters on the edge of uncertainty.

EPILOGUE

Your conscience, the final arbiter, goddess of wisdom, the personification of love and purity. Yes, SOPHIA is all of these things. But who or what is she really? You will come to know the answer when you travel the MYSTIC PATH.

We must travel the road, you and I; it is a long road, for we have many faults. They need to be purged in the fires of earthly life, or we cannot arrive at purity – our destination. It is a long and difficult road, yet it sings with hope and joy,and it shines with the knowledge of truth, and how precious is its beauty.

O, my Soul, I love thee more than I do myself.

For you are beautiful, more beautiful than I can ever know, even more beautiful than the unfolding rose which is your emblem.

And did I not once spurn thee – the stranger at the gate, the traveller on the road, the giver of life.

Did I not once usurp thee, and drive thee from your rightful place.

O, my Soul, forgive me

For you are beautiful, more beautiful than I can ever know

...yes, I have come to love you, my dearest, my cherished one. I restore you to your rightful place, and kneel at your feet. How could I have ever wronged you so, throughout all the ages, I can only be ashamed and distraught. Forgive me Sophia

For you are beautiful, more beautiful than I can ever know.

P.S. A MESSAGE FROM SOPHIA

I am in you, and I am the real you. Nobody can escape from me. Yet you have imprisoned me in a dark lifeless dungeon, and I cry out from my chains: Release me, and give me freedom. Freedom to do the work that I was meant to do, freedom to open the doors of heaven, and bestow its love upon the Earth. But yet I am still imprisoned, saddened by loneliness and your ignorance of me, oppressed by the stifling atmosphere of greed and egotism, the raucous cries and struttings of Ozymandias and false ideologies, lashed by a thousand tongues of hate and intolerance, and tortured in this prison of inactivity by the very ones who were meant to serve me. Release me, and I will guide you. I will give you real life of the spirit, I will show you what Love is, and you will live in my Power and Glory. But perhaps the very reason you have imprisoned me is that you want the glory for yourselves, and try to shield and hide it from me? But think deeply about this.

You are the created one, not the Creator. And nothing can be hidden from me, not even one sparrow's fall.

ADDENDUM:
THE FINAL CHAPTER

WHO AND WHAT IS SOPHIA?

The body has an inner consciousness that is quite apart from us. We, who preen and dance about on the stage, are mere spectators. This inner consciousness uses the laws of chemistry and physics to create the wonders of life, but we have little to do with it. Doctors and biochemists, and other scientific disciplines, study the workings of the body, but even they are only students and spectators at the game. Sophia allows them to play some minor roles, as indeed she encourages the human mind to develop, as she has done for millennia with the body. What is it that keeps us all alive? As stated by the ancient Greeks earth, air, water and fire are all necessary, or as we would put it food, oxygen, water and heat. But although they do indeed maintain life they do not create it. Life, or the life-force, must already be present, there must be consciousness already present, and where does it come from?

It does not come from the brain for that is only part of the body. It does not come from the human mind, for the foregoing applies to most life forms. The power of

Nature and the force of life belong only to Sophia. She alone created the body and the mind. No human being can create life, although they can of course tinker with it; no human being can create one atom or one cell, unless an atom or cell is already present.

We are alive only through the consciousness of Sophia. We live only because she is within us, and our life is maintained by her alone. But do we acknowledge this, or do we deny her very existence and think that we are in charge?

THE ATTRIBUTES OF SOPHIA

Sophia is your subconscious mind, and your conscience.

To the infant science of psychology conscience may appear to be merely a constraint put on the individual by the ethical standards of the era and civilisation in which he happens to live. However it has to be remembered that one psychologist spent years ringing a bell to induce dogs to salivate, for which he received great recognition and plaudits; and yet another seemed to have spent his entire life trying to prove all human beings are obsessed by the sexual impulse! Sophia is infinitely more mature and wiser than that. Her innate moral sense is there to guide us on the path. It is immutable and does not change, whatever emperor or earthly king sits on the throne; it is the civilisation that changes. But the conscience of Sophia is much more than this. It contains the Karmic Book of Life, wherein all is recorded. She herself does not judge or condemn, for eventually we must either own up and make amends – or be erased.

'Nothing can be hidden from me, not even one sparrow's fall.'

How can this be? It is surely not possible. Maybe this is just a bit of religion thrown in to fool us. But do not pass over it lightly for it is a mystical truth. Think deeply about it, and meditate upon it. Sophia knows the answer, indeed Sophia is the answer.

Sophia is also your guardian, and if you always try to stay in contact and rapport with your conscience she will protect you. The synaptic nerves and pathways of the brain are not permanent, although if some of them are constantly visited they will last throughout this present lifetime. However, what is entered into your subconscious mind is permanent and will always be remembered, it cannot be unwritten. It may perhaps be modified by realisations of a more advanced or higher order.

One of Sophia's appellations is that she is the well-spring or fount of Wisdom. She can answer all your questions in absolute Truth.

Questions such as why does Nature often seem red in tooth and claw; why is there such injustice and inequality in the roles we have been given to play? Yes, she knows the answers to all these questions; all you need do is ask, once you have liberated her. Only after you have released her can you hear her answers. You will come to have complete trust and confidence and repose in her, if you successfully complete this journey along the mystic path. You will know things in your heart that you never knew before, treasures not of this world, but pearls of truth and wisdom. You cannot know this truth until you have released Sophia. You cannot release Sophia until you have travelled the mystic path.

Another question we should put to her is this: What small part in the unfolding drama of the human race do you want me to fulfil? For the days of the adolescent idleness and uncaring frivolity are over. It will not be to conquer the world by deeds of anns, nor to rise in political, religious, or industrial power, for these belong to the adolescence of the ego. We begin to sense the maturity and wisdom of Father-Mother Nature in its nurture, care, and love – and have become one with it.

Yet Sophia is still more than this: She is your very soul. Sophia is not only your soul, and my soul: She is the soul of the universe, the force of life, the power of Nature.

'...one day perhaps you will come to love me.'

Yes, my guardian angel, I now know who you are. You have protected and loved me all of my life. You know my every deed, my every word, and even my every thought.

O God, what divine love is this, what tears of joy, what indescribable exquisite wonder fills my heart, this heaven on earth.

A FURTHER MESSAGE FROM SOPHIA

If you have come with me as far as this point then I have something to give you. I cannot give it to you unless you release me. Before another day passes, before another hour, before this moment passes do this for me.

Sit comfortably in a darkened room and relax in calm repose. Close your eyes and withdraw your mind deep into your inner self. Do you sense me there, your inner self, your real self, your divine you. I have waited patiently a long time for this moment, and I love you, and you love me and wish to be one with me. Clasp me with tears of joy, throw open the door, and lead me out into the world, to be one with you from this moment on for evermore, and pray 'I will follow your guidance in all things, for you are the real me, my soul.'

And in return I will give you calmness, tranquillity, and peace profound. I will give you the strength and power of love, a citadel where envy and hate cannot and do not exist.

CONCLUDE

THE DOOR
COME NOT Here Before Your TIME
Before You Are CALLED. For There
Will Be No Admittance

No, they are not physical keys that are needed to open that door, but something intangible, almost magical. LOVE perhaps. But the voice had said 'keys.' Did I need another key then, and what was it? What was my motive for wanting to open the door? To gain power, self-aggrandisement? I realised these thoughts would not unlock the door, but it would open only to those Pure In Heart. And where was the door, it had just been a dream surely? Perhaps I had to dream about it to find it again. I now also knew there was no room on the other side as I first imagined, but a path, the greater Path.

What can I say to you, dear Seeker, before I close, for has it not already been said – in words that will not pass away? I give you my love, and if you love me in return then you are near the Truth. In this technological and scientific age the path may seem obscured and difficult to find, but there is a Path, it has always been there and always will be – *Noble, Pure in Heart, Loving* – we will tread it together, you and I, I and you, we who are one.